the further adventures of

SHERLOCK HOLMES

THE MAN FROM HELL

AVAILABLE NOW FROM TITAN BOOKS

THE FURTHER ADVENTURES OF SHERLOCK HOLMES
THE ECTOPLASMIC MAN
Daniel Stashower
ISBN: 9781848564923

THE FURTHER ADVENTURES OF SHERLOCK HOLMES
THE SCROLL OF THE DEAD
David Stuart Davies
ISBN: 9781848564930

THE FURTHER ADVENTURES OF SHERLOCK HOLMES
THE STALWART COMPANIONS
H. Paul Jeffers
ISBN: 9781848565098

THE FURTHER ADVENTURES OF SHERLOCK HOLMES
THE VEILED DETECTIVE
David Stuart Davies
ISBN: 9781848564909

THE FURTHER ADVENTURES OF SHERLOCK HOLMES
THE WAR OF THE WORLDS
Manly W. Wellman & Wade Wellman
ISBN: 9781848564916

the further adventures of

SHERLOCK HOLMES

THE MAN FROM HELL

BARRIE ROBERTS

TITAN BOOKS

THE FURTHER ADVENTURES OF SHERLOCK HOLMES
THE MAN FROM HELL

ISBN: 9781848565081

Published by
Titan Books
A division of Titan Publishing Group Ltd.
144 Southwark St
London
SE1 0UP

First edition: February 2010
10 9 8 7 6 5 4 3 2

Names, places and incidents are either products of the author's
imagination or are used fictitiously. Any resemblance to actual persons,
living or dead (except for satirical purposes), is entirely coincidental.

© 1997, 2010 Barrie Roberts

Visit our website:
www.titanbooks.com

What did you think of this book? We love to hear from our readers.
Please email us at: readerfeedback@titanemail.com, or write to us at
the above address. To receive advance information, news,
competitions, and exclusive Titan offers online, please register as a
member by clicking the 'sign up' button on our website:
www.titanbooks.com

Printed and bound in the USA.

Foreword

The circumstances in which I came into possession of what seems to be a quantity of manuscripts by the late Dr John H. Watson have been explained in an earlier publication – *Sherlock Holmes and the Railway Maniac*. Briefly, they appear to have been in the possession of my maternal grandfather, who was both a medical man and a contemporary of Watson's in the RAMC.

In preparing the present manuscript for publication I have made such checks as have occured to me, to try and confirm its authenticity. The results of my researches will be found in a series of notes appended to the narrative. Suffice it to say, at this point, that I am as satisfied as I can be that this is a case of Sherlock Holmes' recorded by his partner, Dr Watson, of which nothing was formerly known, apart from a couple of passing references in the Doctor's published records.

Barrie Roberts
1996

One

The Death Of A Philanthropist

In looking over the many records I have prepared of the cases of my friend Mr Sherlock Holmes, I find that I have not given his followers an account of the Backwater murders. That I did not do so earlier was for two reasons. In part it was because the story is one that embraces both appalling cruelty and corruption. In addition it was to avoid embarrassment to the living and to prevent the circulation of information which the ill-disposed would readily use to besmirch the memory of one of the Empire's greatest philanthropists. Indeed, my use of the pseudonym Backwater is still necessary, for the principal victim in that unhappy affair bore a name which may yet be read on memorial plaques and on the foundation stones of charitable institutes across the nation. Nevertheless, the resolution of the case was one which afforded my friend Sherlock Holmes no little satisfaction and removed a deep-rooted and secret evil from our public life, and so this manuscript has been prepared with due consideration for the privacy of those involved, while setting out the essential facts of the case.

My journal shows that it was the early summer of 1886 when the

Backwater matter came to Holmes' attention. It was during the first period of our shared residence at Baker Street and I had become well aware of the irregular habits of my companion. Despite my lack of an occupation, I endeavoured to maintain a fairly orderly regime, but my efforts were brought to nothing by the moods of my friend. If I rose early it would be to find that he had not been to bed, or that he had slept late and would take his breakfast at an hour more suitable for luncheon. Yet when the exigencies of a case demanded it, he would rise early and alert and set out about his business.

There were mornings when he surprised both Mrs Hudson and me by being early at the breakfast table when he had no enquiry in hand. On those days he seemed to expect action and would go through the newspapers thoroughly and read his post as though a summons was imminent. If the papers or the post showed no indications, and if no prospective client's foot had been heard on our stair by mid-morning, he would take himself off to the British Museum to pursue his arcane researches into early British charters or ancient languages. I came to believe that this behaviour derived from an excess of energy at the completion of a successful case, and I noted with misgivings that the phenomenon disappeared when he took to poisoning himself with cocaine.

It was one such morning when the Backwater case began, a bright morning when the sun struck deep into our little sitting-room. Holmes' early rising had not taken Mrs Hudson by surprise and, having finished breakfast, he turned over the newspapers.

'Lord Backwater has been murdered!' I exclaimed, seeing a notice to that effect in my paper.

'So I see,' said Holmes from behind his own newspaper, 'and one paper has a leader arguing that it is evidence of a completely disordered and unjust universe that a man who has given employment to thousands, hugely enriched the nation and has never stinted in his donations to the unfortunate should be struck down by poachers.'

'Is that what occurred?' I asked. 'There are few details here.'

'There are longer accounts in some of the papers,' said my friend. 'It seems that he was strolling in his own park when he disturbed poachers about their work and was savagely attacked.'

'Then it has no interest for you?' I asked. 'Despite the man's wealth and eminence?'

Holmes eyed me over the top of his newspaper. 'I am surprised,' he said, 'that you do not appear to realise that the personality or antecedents of a victim are of interest only insofar as they may reveal the motive for a crime. If the police in the West Country are correct then it is of no significance that it was Lord Backwater who disturbed a band of poachers; they would just as readily have murdered you or me.'

'It seems a very cold-blooded attitude to me,' I admitted.

He laughed shortly. 'Would you consider a patient's personality or history when treating his wounds, Doctor? If they did not assist your diagnosis or affect your treatment? No, Watson, you treat the diseases of the individual and I treat the irruptions of society and neither of us can allow our approach to be clouded by sentiment, however worthy.'

He flung his newspaper into the seat of the basket-chair and drained his coffee. Standing up, he stretched his long, lean frame and sauntered over to the sunlit window. The morning deliveries had been made and the day's business had not yet begun, so that the street was quiet, apart from the rattle of a solitary cab. 'You may abandon the newspapers,' he said. 'There is nothing there of interest.'

'It is what journalists call "the silly season", Holmes,' I ventured.

'A gross misrepresentation!' he snapped. 'There is a world of difference between silliness and the arrant imbecilities that obsess the whole of Fleet Street at present. The established press comforts itself and its readers with the information that nothing of any consequence has changed since yesterday – regarding this as "news"! The radical papers treat the same facts as evidence of a stagnant society and the popular sheets invent and repeat unprovable assertions about the private life of the Queen's family! Rubbish! All of it!'

'I had thought that the items about the Duchess–' I began, but he cut me short.

'...might once have produced an interesting commission for us,' he growled, 'but that is no longer likely when the lady's indiscretions are the common tattle of every Bermondsey barmaid!'

He stared moodily out of the window, evidently disappointed that he had risen early to no purpose.

'I believe,' he said, after a moment, 'that we have some early business. What do you make of the couple across the street?'

I joined him at the window and followed his pointing finger. On the opposite pavement stood two gentlemen who had just dismounted from a cab.

'The younger man is dressed both discreetly and expensively. He stands back while the older man pays the cabby. I surmise that the elder of the two, who is dressed in a more workaday fashion, is some senior assistant to the younger – perhaps a man of business, a lawyer – and the other is a man of some wealth.'

I turned to Holmes, pleased with my observations, but he was still gazing down through the window.

'You might have observed,' he chided, 'that both are in mourning. Tell me, what do you make of the bags?'

'The bags?' I repeated, and looked again. The pair were now looking across to our building and, as I watched, they picked up their baggage and started across the deserted street.

'The younger carries only a small Gladstone, while the elder carries a similar, though shabbier, bag and what seems to be a document case. I believe that confirms my earlier impression.'

'I was referring,' said Holmes, 'to the bags at the knees of their trousers. I have remarked on other occasions that the hands are the most informative area when dealing with craftsmen, clerks and labourers, but that more may be learned from the trousers of the middle and upper classes. Here, as you rightly deduced, are a gentleman of position in expensive mourning clothes and his man of business in good office black, yet both have allowed their trousers to become distended at the knee. Can you not imagine a reason?'

I confessed that I could not and he drew out his watch.

'The Great Western Express,' he said, 'arrived in London only minutes ago, yet we have two visitors who have taken the first cab on the Paddington rank and hurried straight to our doorstep without pausing for so much as a cup of tea.'

'But what has that to do with their trousers?' I asked, mystified. 'And how can you say that they have travelled by the Western Express?'

'Had they travelled overnight they would have occupied sleeping compartments. They have travelled early this morning, seated face to face in a carriage, and have leant forward to discuss at length some matter of great urgency, thereby causing the bags to which I drew your attention. They might have come from East Anglia, the Midlands or the South Coast, but the timing of their arrival indicates a fast cab from the Great Western terminus. If I shared your love of gambling Watson, I would wager you a sovereign that our bell is now being rung by the new Viscount Backwater and, I suspect, his solicitor.'

I had already learned not to doubt my friend's extraordinary inferences and, within minutes, they were confirmed when Mrs Hudson announced Lord Backwater and his solicitor.

A Cryptic Note

'Colonel Caddage's views on my father's death are completely erroneous!' exclaimed Lord Backwater.

Our guests were seated and Mrs Hudson had replenished the coffee. The new Lord Backwater was evidently deeply agitated.

'And who, pray, is Colonel Caddage?' enquired Holmes.

'He is our Chief Constable,' said Mr Predge, the solicitor.

'And he insists on treating my father's murder as a casual act by poachers when it is evidently something else!' asserted the young Lord.

Holmes raised a hand to stop the angry young man. 'Perhaps it would be better if you were to give me the facts of your father's death, Lord Backwater, without applying any interpretation. Then we shall see where they lead us.'

'You are right, of course,' said Lord Backwater and paused to collect his thoughts.

'My father left our home on the afternoon before last at about four. He gave no indication that he would be absent from dinner but he had not returned by dinner-time. My sister and I grew alarmed and ordered a search for him. His body was found in the beech woods to the south

12

of the house. He had been brutally beaten to death.'

Lord Backwater shuddered slightly and relapsed into silence. Holmes sat for a moment with his head tilted back and his eyes half closed without speaking.

'The newspapers,' he said, without opening his eyes, 'give that account, but no more. Was your father in any way distressed or disturbed before he left the house?'

'I did not see him that afternoon,' said Lord Backwater, 'but my sister reports that he was in good spirits and intended to walk no further than a particularly ancient beech tree. It was one of his favourite walks.'

'The late Lord Backwater was celebrated for two things if one can believe the accounts in the newspapers,' said Holmes. 'He had given large sums to charity and he was notably reclusive. Is that so?'

'He had donated hundreds of thousands to worthy causes,' said the young man, 'but he eschewed any form of notoriety. Almost his entire life was passed within the bounds of the estate. He hardly ever visited the county town and only went to London very occasionally on business matters.'

'So that a stranger who wished to make a personal appeal to his charity might seek to waylay him on a familiar walk?' queried Holmes.

'Ha!' exclaimed His Lordship. 'Already you see another explanation.'

'I see only what you tell me,' said Holmes, 'and I examine all the possible meanings of these data. Do not allow yourself to be misled by my questions, though you may rest assured that poachers are unlikely culprits.'

'I was quite sure of that,' said Lord Backwater.

'I am certain. The time of day is wrong, the proximity to Backwater Hall is wrong, and because poachers would have fled or hidden rather than launch an unnecessary attack upon an elderly man. Do you have some other reason for your view?' asked Holmes, and he opened his eyes wide.

The young man faltered slightly before my friend's gaze. 'I have…
I have… a note which my father received.'

Mr Predge opened his document case and passed his client an
envelope. Lord Backwater gave it to Holmes without opening it.

My friend turned the envelope over in his hands and I could see
that it was of cheap white paper. Across the front a firm hand had
written "Lord Backwater, Backwater Hall" in ink. It had been sealed
but bore no postage stamp.

Holmes' long fingers extracted a single sheet of paper from within
the envelope and he held it up to the light.

'A quarto sheet of cheap writing-paper,' he mused. 'No watermark,
a poor pen-nib and a diluted ink.'

He lowered the paper and examined its message, which consisted
of only a few words:

The man from the Gates of Hell will be at the old place at six.

There was no signature.

'This was written,' said Holmes, 'by a man of moderate education
and vigorous nature, probably in his middle years. The paper, pen
and inks suggest a post office, hotel or inn, but if it had been written
at a post office it would, most probably, have been stamped. Did your
father have any Welsh connections?'

'I do not think so,' said Lord Backwater, but he looked to his solicitor
for confirmation. The lawyer shook his head.

'And does the expression "the Gates of Hell" mean anything to either
of you?' Holmes enquired.

Now they both shook their heads.

'Then it may be the other Gates of Hell,' said Holmes. 'What about
the phrase "the old place"?'

'It means nothing to me,' said Lord Backwater. 'I have told you that my father frequently strolled to that particular ancient beech tree.'

'When did your father receive this note?' asked Holmes.

'It seems to have been on the afternoon before his death,' said the young man. 'It lay on his desk that night and both my sister and I had been in the room during the morning and it was not there.'

'Was anyone seen to call at the house in the afternoon?'

'No, Mr Holmes, but I am not able to say that no one did.'

'Then it is at least possible that it was delivered that day,' said Holmes. 'Why have you not given this to the police?'

'But I showed it to Colonel Caddage!' exclaimed Lord Backwater. 'He told me that, since I could not explain it and since we could not swear to its delivery, it was irrelevant – a coincidence that undoubtedly had some innocent explanation!'

The lawyer nodded in confirmation. 'It was at that point that I began to agree with Lord Backwater that a more vigorous investigation was required. A wire to my London agents gave me your name and we came at once,' he said.

'You were quite right," said Holmes, 'to consult someone who has always believed that there is a great deal too much coincidence about.

'Lord Backwater,' he continued, 'the newspapers list some of the causes to which your father contributed over the years. Most were concerned with the education of the poor, the relief of poverty or the care of orphans. Did he contribute to animal charities?'

'As you may imagine,' said Mr Predge, 'the late Lord Backwater received many appeals to his generosity. The causes you have mentioned were foremost, but he made regular donations to support organisations that cared for horses.'

'He was not a dog lover?' asked Holmes.

'He neither liked nor disliked them. There are dogs about the estate,' said Lord Backwater, 'working dogs, and old Towler followed my father about.'

'But neither old Towler nor any other dog was with him when he met his death?'

'No sir,' said the young Lord, and a slow light of remembrance dawned across his face.

'What have you recalled?' demanded my friend.

'The dogs,' said Lord Backwater slowly. 'There have been a number of occasions recently when my father has ordered the dogs locked up before he went out for a walk, as he did that afternoon.'

Holmes smiled, but quickly suppressed the expression. 'I fear,' he said, 'that I must ask a question that may appear indelicate in the circumstances. The newspapers say that Lady Backwater has been dead some ten years—"

'Mr Holmes!' interrupted Lord Backwater angrily. 'Do not dare to suggest that my father went to meet a — a female! My father and mother were devoted to each other and since her death he has not looked at another woman.'

'It was a remote possibility in the light of the note,' said Holmes, 'but it had to be considered. Now that it has been eliminated, we may, I think, draw some inferences.'

Lord Backwater and Mr Predge leaned forward eagerly.

'It seems likely that the note was, in fact, delivered by hand to Backwater Hall on the afternoon of your father's death,' said Holmes. 'The fact that no one saw it delivered is not evidence against the proposition. That an action was unremarked does not make it impossible. The note seems to be from someone with a long-standing acquaintance with your father, if not friendship.'

'Why do you say so?' asked Lord Backwater.

'Because your father accepted the assignation in the note and went to it without trepidation and with no precautions. Evidently he felt that he had nothing to fear from the meeting.'

'Then he was killed by someone that he knew!' exclaimed the young Viscount.

'I did not say so, nor do I believe it to be so,' said Holmes. 'You are in danger, Lord Backwater, of running ahead of the available data. Tell me, had your father any enemies?'

'None of which I was aware,' said the young man, and turned again to his lawyer for confirmation.

'The late Lord Backwater,' said the solicitor, 'was universally admired and respected. Apart from those major acts of charity which became known to the public, he made many minor donations to relieve distress in individual cases in the area of Backwater Hall. In addition, he was scrupulous in his commercial transactions, often to his own disadvantage.'

Holmes nodded. 'I see,' he said. 'Then there is only one more question of consequence. What connection had Lord Backwater with the Antipodes?'

Lord Backwater and his solicitor looked at each other with identical expressions of astonishment. Even I, who had become used, I thought, to my friend's apparent non-sequiturs, was bewildered.

'None, none, I think,' said the young Lord. 'He had business interests, of course, in many regions – in America, in Canada, in South America, South Africa – but you will have read that in the obituaries. I do not think he had any interest in the Antipodes, had he, Mr Predge?'

'I am sure not,' said the lawyer. 'His fortune came from the mining of metals and gems and, as Lord Patrick has said, his holdings were widespread, but I cannot recall any connection with Australia or New Zealand.'

'You said that you had only that one question,' said Lord Backwater. 'Does that mean that you have reached a conclusion, Mr Holmes?'

'I understand your concern to bring your father's murderers to justice,' said Holmes, 'but it is far too early for conclusions. Inferences, yes. We can be reasonably sure that your father left home in a cheerful frame of mind to meet an acquaintance – perhaps even a friend – who disliked or was afraid of dogs and whom your father did not regard as a threat. In keeping that rendezvous he was set upon and savagely killed.'

'Then you believe his friend – his acquaintance – lured him into a trap?' asked Lord Backwater.

'I do not know,' said Holmes. 'At this point I cannot be certain, but I believe it improbable. It seems to me much more likely that the trap was set by others, for one or both of them. No doubt we shall learn more when we accompany you to Backwater Hall.'

He rose and our guests rose too. 'When shall you be there?' asked Lord Backwater.

Holmes glanced at the mantel clock. 'I have no engagements that require me to remain in town,' he said. 'If Mr Predge will be kind enough to reserve a first-class smoker, Watson and I will meet you at Paddington in time for the noon train. Good day, Lord Backwater. Good day, Mr Predge.'

When the visitors had departed, Holmes flung himself full length on the couch with a hand over his eyes. 'Be so good,' he asked me, 'as to run over the longest obituary you can find for me.'

I shuffled through the mass of the morning's papers and finally selected a lengthy obituary of the late Viscount Backwater and rehearsed the principal points for Holmes.

'Former James Lisle – born in humble circumstances – orphaned at an early age – took to the sea – adventurous years in America – one of the discoverers of the Great Empress Silver Lode – expanding interests in mining – returned to England twenty-five years ago – reclusive life at Backwater – increasing generosity to charities – made Viscount

Backwater – married Lady Felicia Eaglestone – wife dead ten years – leaves a son Patrick, the new Viscount, and daughter Patricia, engaged to Henry Ruthen.' I looked up at Holmes. 'There seems to be little else of consequence,' I said.

Holmes waved his hand impatiently. 'It is not there, it is not there!' he exclaimed.

'What is it you are seeking?' I asked.

'The Antipodean connection,' he snapped.

'It is the entry to this maze and we must find it.'

'But why are you so certain that there is such a connection?' I enquired.

'Because it is in the note,' he replied, and swung his long legs off the couch. 'Be so good as to ring for our boots, Watson. We have an appointment at Paddington.'

Three

THE TATTOOED CORPSE

Our journey to the west was pursued largely in silence. Both Lord Backwater and his lawyer were showing signs of the strain under which the tragedy and their hurried journey to London had placed them and it was impossible for me to question Holmes as to his remarks at Baker Street.

Wiggin, Lord Backwater's principal gamekeeper, met us at Backwater Halt with a carriage, but also present was an Inspector of Police who greeted Holmes warmly.

'Mr Holmes,' he said, 'when I heard that Lord Backwater had gone to consult you I was very pleased, sir, very pleased indeed.' I was intrigued to note that the accent was from the lowlands of Scotland rather than these western valleys.

'Scott!' exclaimed Holmes, smiling warmly. 'The move west has evidently been successful.' He turned to me and introduced the officer. 'Watson,' he said, 'this high official of the County Police was a mere constable back in my Montague Street days, when I had the opportunity to assist his division with a small matter. I take it,' he said to the

Inspector, 'that you are not in agreement with your Chief Constable's view of the matter?'

'That is not for me to say, sir. Let us just say that I am pleased to see you here, Mr Holmes.'

Holmes turned to our client. 'I shall ask Inspector Scott to take Dr Watson and me to the scene of the crime, Lord Backwater, but there is no need for you to attend. Perhaps we may wait on you at Backwater Hall later, when I may have some observations for you.'

The Viscount's relief was evident. 'That is most thoughtful of you, Mr Holmes. We shall take your luggage on and await your findings.'

Very shortly Wiggin took Lord Backwater and his solicitor away and Holmes turned to Inspector Scott.

'Now,' he said, 'we may address ourselves to that most unpleasant but necessary of speculations, Inspector. Is there any likelihood that Lord Patrick, or any other member of the family, is involved in this matter?'

'I should say not,' said the Inspector. 'Not that it can be entirely ruled out, but as far as I can determine relations between the family were most amicable.'

'Then, if you do not have violent poachers in these parts, we had best find another explanation,' said Holmes. 'Is it possible to see the body?'

'It is, Mr Holmes,' said Scott. 'It is at the county mortuary for the present. The Chief Constable was all for releasing it to the family, but once I heard you were on your way I knew you would wish to examine it.'

The station trap took us to the little red-brick county mortuary buildings where we were soon examining the corpse of a well-built, healthy man in his fifties. His early days had left him with fine muscular development and he had not run to fat in his retirement.

The front upper portion of the body and both arms were covered with the marks of vicious cudgel blows, while the cause of death was easy to see in a single, massive blow struck to the back of the head. It was plain that Lord Backwater had defended himself vigorously against more than one assailant before being felled from behind.

Inspector Scott and the attendant rolled the body into a prone position and, as the back was revealed, Holmes drew a long breath and smiled slightly as though some unspoken prediction had proved true.

I was astonished, for the pallor of death had made more visible on the dead man's back a pattern of old and wide scars.

'He was flogged!' I exclaimed. 'More than once by the look of it!'

'So I perceive,' said Holmes, 'but can your military eye help me as to whether this was done in the Army or Navy?'

'No,' I said, after a second look. 'I've seen any number of old sweats who've been triangled. Their marks are higher than these, care being taken in the services to avoid the kidneys. This man was lashed at random by someone, most probably in his youth.'

'Excellent, Watson,' said Holmes and signalled to have the cadaver restored to its former position. 'Now, what do you make of his tattoos?'

'Very little,' I replied. 'We know that he was humbly raised and worked in mines. Many such men carry tattoos.'

'Not such as these,' said my friend, and stepping back towards the table he turned the corpse's left forearm slightly outwards.

I had noted that there was a tattoo on the inner side of the forearm, but I had paid it scant attention during my examination. Now I looked more closely and saw that it was amateur work of the kind that is done by schoolboys with a pen-nib and ink, or by soldiers with a knife-point and gunpowder, but it had been strongly and regularly incised and stood out clearly against the pallor of the skin.

It was none of the patterns that I had ever seen in the Army or in my civilian practice. It consisted of a heraldic cross-pattée with a single word in capitals across its centre – "NEVER".

My face must have shown my bewilderment, for Holmes turned the right forearm as well. There, in the matching position, was another such decoration, this time a simple square containing the word 'EVER'.

'Do they tell you anything?' Holmes demanded.

'Very little, Holmes,' I admitted. 'They are not professional work, but that means little. Soldiers, sailors, even public schoolboys tattoo themselves and each other.'

'Schoolboy tattoos are made with common ink,' said Holmes, 'while soldiers and sailors use gunpowder. Both fade relatively quickly. Sometimes lampblack is used and that can last a lifetime. I think that is the agent here.'

He turned the two forearms again, gazing thoughtfully at the inscriptions.

'It is a pity,' he remarked, 'that they are not on the torso or the upper arm.'

'Why so?' I enquired.

'The growth of the body and the development of the muscles would have distorted them had they been applied at an early age, but no such distortion occurs on the inner forearm. What do you learn from the symbols themselves?'

'I have seen a deal of tattoos,' I said, 'but I recall none like these. Soldiers have swords, guns, regimental emblems; sailors have the anchor of faith and the crown of hope, ships, ships' names, mermaids; both have hearts, flags, inscriptions to sweethearts, wives and mothers. I even remember attending a fellow on the *Orontes* who had the famous fox-chase tattoo.'

'Well done, Watson!' exclaimed Holmes. 'I see that you have retained a little of my oft-repeated observations on the importance of tattoos. Professor Lombroso asserts that all tattoos are the hallmark of a criminal personality, but in that, as in so many other matters, he is wrong. Continental criminals may have misled him by their flamboyant tattoos. British criminals occasionally wear a small emblem of their particular gang, often on the edge of the left palm, where it is unobtrusive and readily covered by the thumb, and a very few wear emblems of their criminous trade, but in general they conform to the ordinary decorations of the lower classes.'

'Then what do these mean?' I asked, indicating Lord Backwater's tattoos.

'They mean', he said, lifting each arm in turn, 'on the cross – never, and on the square – ever.'

'An expression of affection and loyalty,' I said. 'Surely the name of a sweetheart should be with them?'

Holmes chuckled mirthlessly. 'There is little affection embodied in that oath,' he said, 'and it was directed to no female.'

'A secret society?' I hazarded. 'Do they signify that Lord Backwater was a criminal?'

'No,' said my friend, 'but they signify that the late Lord Backwater's past was more varied than the obituarists imagined, and they confirm my view that the man from the Gates of Hell came from precisely that address.'

Four

THE COCKNEY AGENT

Holmes and I waited at the roadside as Inspector Scott gave instructions to the mortuary-keeper about the release of Lord Backwater's body to the family. As we did so, a rattle of wheels and hooves heralded the appearance of a smartly painted landau pulled by two fine greys. The driver brought his animals to a halt close to us and his passenger sprang to the ground almost before the vehicle had halted.

The newcomer was an exceedingly tall individual who, despite the warmth of the day, wore a long, old-fashioned military frock-coat, curiously frogged and braided. His narrow, square-chinned features were set with two protuberant black eyes and he carried his chin high.

'Scott!' he roared at the Police Inspector. 'Is one of these two fellows the Cockney agent?' and he jerked a heavy, gold-mounted cane towards Holmes and me.

Before the embarrassed Inspector could reply, Holmes stepped forward. 'I believe,' he said, 'that I am the person you seek. My name is Sherlock Holmes and this is my companion, Dr Watson.'

The stranger looked us up and down with an arrogant stare.

'I,' he said, 'am the Chief Constable of this county. What, Holmes, makes you believe that your presence here is of any value?'

'I merely answer the call of those who claim my assistance,' said my friend. 'In this case Lord Patrick was moved to travel urgently to London and consult me. He revealed to me aspects of the case which intrigued me and which I believed would bear closer investigation.'

'"Aspects of the case"!' snorted the Chief Constable. 'There is only one aspect of the case that matters. A generous and decent man – a friend and neighbour of mine as well – has been ruthlessly struck down by poaching rabble. The perpetrators shall hang for it at the next assize and it will need no Cockney amateur to guide my officers in tracking them. Oh, I understand Lord Patrick's concern that everything possible should be done, but mark me, Holmes, if you interfere with my officers in the least particular I shall run you out of the county. We need no townees here – this is a simple country matter!'

'I hear what you say,' said Holmes from between narrowed lips, 'and you need have no fear that I shall impede your investigation. On the contrary, I will tell you now that this is not a simple country matter confined to this pleasant county. The origins of Lord Backwater's death must be sought a good deal further away.'

Colonel Caddage stared silently at my friend for a moment, then 'Deluded!' he snarled. 'Melodramatic poppycock intended to increase your fees!' and he turned back to his carriage. As he clambered in he roared again at the Inspector, 'When you've finished wasting your time with these fellows, kindly remember I shall expect your usual report!'

As the landau rattled away Holmes turned to the mortified Inspector. 'Do not apologise,' he said. 'It is I who should apologise that I thought your move westward an advancement, but I had not then met your Chief Constable.'

'Chief Constables come in all shapes and manners,' said Scott, 'and this one can't forget he was in the Army. I pity the poor beggars that served under him. At the worst I can resign.'

'Was that his usual manner?' I asked.

'He did not like the idea of your being called in,' said the Inspector. 'He feels it an affront to his force. When he's angry he either shouts and threatens or he turns sarcastic. I dare say I shall hear a deal of sarcasm at your expense when I make my nightly report. What shall I tell him, Mr Holmes?'

'Tell him what you wish, Inspector,' replied Holmes. 'My enquiries are not secret from the official Police. If Colonel Caddage prefers to reject the fruit of them that is his affair.'

We had climbed aboard the station trap and Inspector Scott explained that he was taking us to the scene of the crime. 'I recall your remarks on the value of the place as evidence and I have had it roped off and a constable set by,' he said, and earned an approving nod from Holmes.

Our road took us into old woodland, richly green and deeply shaded at this season. 'All in front of us is part of Lord Backwater's land,' Inspector Scott explained. 'The Chief Constable's estate is smaller and lies to our left.'

He halted the trap at one point, where a break in the woods revealed a distant view of Backwater Hall. I was aware that Lord Backwater had purchased an existing estate upon his return to England and I had expected that the Hall would be Tudor, perhaps, or at the latest Georgian. To my surprise the building that lay across the meadows to our right was of relatively recent design, though a handsome house in its own right.

'I had thought Backwater Hall was an ancient building,' I remarked.

'The old Hall was Tudor, I believe,' said the Inspector, 'but the locals say that when Lord Backwater bought the estate he had the old Hall burned to the ground and built this new one. The old house stood there, nearer to the road,' he said, pointing.

'What an extraordinary thing to do,' I said.

'Lord Backwater was a man who liked everything up to date,' said Inspector Scott. 'The new house had all the latest inventions from America. It has electric lighting everywhere, even in the skivvies' rooms, a cold store, even telegraph instruments. I dare say he simply wanted to start afresh.'

We continued on our way until we reached a green track into the Backwater estate. Here we dismounted and followed the Police Officer along the track until we came to one end of a row of magnificent old beeches. The long glade pierced the woodlands from the track where we stood to the open meadows that sloped away to Backwater Hall. The ancient trunks stood like grey Norman pillars and the afternoon sun on the canopy of young leaves above cast a pale green glow through the glade.

Inspector Scott led us down the row until we reached one particularly large tree near the far end. It had a wide, scarred trunk, rising about eight feet before it branched out wide and high. A rope barrier supported on iron stakes had been erected around the tree and a few feet from it. Beneath the next tree sat a young constable who sprang to his feet and saluted Inspector Scott.

'Good afternoon, sir,' he said. 'All in order here, I think.'

'I hope so, for your sake,' said Scott. 'This is Mr Sherlock Holmes, the consulting detective, and this is his friend Dr Watson, Constable. You would do well to watch Mr Holmes and observe how he addresses a problem.'

He turned to Holmes. 'We've had no rain, Mr Holmes, and I secured the ground as soon as the body was removed. I hope there is material for you.'

'I am sure of it, Inspector,' said Holmes, and stepped up to the rope. For a few moments he scanned the ground inside the barrier and the trunk of the tree. Then he paced around the roped perimeter, never taking his eyes off the ground. At last he ducked under the rope.

Even I could see that the moss around the old tree's roots and the roots themselves had been hacked and scarred by boots, but Holmes seemed barely to glance at these marks. Instead he would stoop now and then, draw his lens from his pocket and apply it closely to areas of the moss. At one point he descended to his hands and knees, casting continually about the mossy ground with his lens in one hand, while the fingers of the other traced something on the ground. He seemed like nothing so much as a great dark hound, seeking the scent of some other creature on the forest floor.

When he had been twice around the bole of the beech, and had examined that too, to head height and beyond, he pocketed his glass, brushed down his clothing and ducked under the rope.

'Do you find any indications?' enquired Scott.

'I find more than indications,' said Holmes. 'I find clear evidence of what occurred here. Your preservation of that evidence has enabled me to learn much.'

All of us looked at him expectantly and he continued, 'Three men came on foot from the same direction as ourselves. Two were heavy-set men in strong working boots, one was lighter and wore old, broken boots. They came well in advance of their prey and concealed themselves behind the tree. While they waited they rolled cigarettes. The tobacco, which was a coarse American variety, was held in a pouch by one of the heavy-set pair, but the match was struck by his lighter companion who was left-handed.'

The young constable was staring at Holmes in frank amazement and I was moved to protest. 'Holmes!' I exclaimed. 'I can see how you deduced much of this from the footmarks, but the tobacco pouch and the left-handedness are too much!'

'You know my methods, Watson, but you do not apply them,' Holmes replied. 'As you remark, much of my information comes from the footprints, including the left-handedness. The match was struck against the tree-trunk and the striker's foot pressed into the moss close to the trunk. It was his left foot, *ergo* he struck with his left hand. The slight spillages of tobacco as it was handed around show where each stood and which held the pouch. Now, may I continue with my remarks?'

I made no further interruption as he explained how the three had stubbed out their cigarettes on seeing Lord Backwater approach across the meadows and had lurked behind the great tree as the nobleman waited for his visitor.

'And that,' said Holmes, 'establishes one important fact.'

'What is that?' I asked.

'That they had no interest in Lord Backwater, but waited for the Man from Hell,' said the Inspector.

'Precisely,' responded my friend and continued his narrative. 'Lord Backwater waited a few minutes and lit a cigar. He paced this side of the tree and he stood and examined the initials carved on the trunk. Then he became aware of his visitor approaching across the meadows and he walked to the edge of the wood.'

He pointed with his stick towards the meadow then went on, 'Together they returned to this tree, where they stood in conversation. At that point two of the ambushers sprang upon them.'

He paused. 'A fierce struggle ensued, but Lord Backwater was eventually struck down from behind. If he was not their intended prey, it is probable that his death confused them momentarily, allowing the stranger to make his escape across the meadow. The murderers were unwilling to pursue him in open country and retreated the way they had come.'

He fell silent and I offered him a cigarette. Inspector Scott turned to his constable. 'Let that be a lesson to you,' he said, 'in the importance of preserving every trace of evidence at the scene of a crime.'

With Holmes' permission the constable was left to remove the rope fence and we made our way back to the trap. As we boarded, the Inspector asked, 'Is there anything more that you wish to know before I leave you at Backwater Hall, Mr Holmes?'

'If you know it,' said Holmes, 'I would be grateful for the name of Colonel Caddage's hedger and ditcher.'

The police officer looked as confused as me. 'Why,' he said, 'it's a mad old creature known as Tin-Fiddle Williams.'

'And where might I find him?' asked Holmes.

'On a Saturday night you will find him in the tap-room of the Backwater Arms, playing his tin fiddle, but otherwise he has a shack on the Colonel's land. I will point out the path as we pass.'

On the way to Backwater Hall the Inspector showed us a green ride that led into the Chief Constable's estate. 'About a half-mile up there,' he said, 'is a path to the right that leads down to a pool. Tin-Fiddle's shack is at the bottom of that path, but I would not let Colonel Caddage catch you on his land.'

'Never fear,' said Holmes. 'I have no such intention.'

As he left us at our client's door the Inspector asked one last question. 'I have to report to the Colonel,' he said. 'What may I tell him, Mr Holmes?'

'You may tell him,' said Holmes, 'everything that I have observed and deduced, but you should emphasise that they are merely the views of a Cockney agent.'

Five

TIN-FIDDLE WILLIAMS

We lodged that night at the Hall, where Holmes outlined to Lord Backwater his discoveries in the beech glade. The young nobleman had theories of his own, most particularly that the stranger who met his father had led him into a trap.

'It remains possible,' admitted Holmes, 'but I am far more ready to believe that the exercise was designed to trap and kill your father's visitor.'

'Then why did he escape?' demanded Lord Backwater. 'Why did he not stay and assist my father?'

'The blow that felled your father was instantaneously fatal, and obviously so,' said Holmes. 'There was nothing further to be done for him and his death left his visitor outnumbered two-to-one which is, no doubt, why he disengaged himself and made off across the meadows.'

'I still believe the stranger was part of the plot,' said Lord Backwater, and on that unresolved note the conversation ended.

After breakfast the next morning, Holmes invited me to join him on a visit to Tin-Fiddle Williams. We walked the road between the two estates and readily found the grassy ride which Inspector Scott had shown us. Here and there along its length we caught glimpses through the trees of a large pool fringed with reeds.

At length we came to a footpath leading towards the water. It was a narrow track, winding closely under the trees, sometimes skirting rotted stumps and occasionally crossed by twisted roots. The trees in full leaf above darkened the path and we had to pick our way carefully.

After about another half-mile we came to a point where the path opened out on to a wide tree-covered slope, running down to the edge of the lake. To our right stood a grotesque shanty. It seemed to me that it might once have been a shooting hut, but it had been repaired and extended with a wide variety of materials from galvanised iron sheets to enamelled railway advertisements and the panels of tea-chests. A part of the roof was formed from a flattened tin bath and the chimney, which smoked fitfully, was a section of cast drainpipe.

'It seems we have found Mr Williams at home,' remarked my friend, pointing with his stick to the smoke, and we approached the only door we could see in the shack. It was made from rough planks and bore a railway company's enamelled warnings that trespassers made themselves liable to imprisonment or transportation.

Sherlock Holmes rapped on the boards with the handle of his stick and, after a pause, the door opened by inches. A lean face, darkened by soot and weather, appeared and two watery, red-rimmed eyes surveyed us from either side of a craggy nose.

'Have I the pleasure of addressing Mr Tin-Fiddle Williams?' asked Holmes cheerily.

'Who wants to know?' grunted the door-keeper.

Holmes gave him our names and added, 'I am a fellow musician who has heard of your remarkable instrument and hoped that I might see it.'

Holmes had held up a coin and the old man took it without a word and pulled the door wide, standing back to admit us to his unique dwelling. We stepped into the shanty and stood in the middle of what seemed to be its principal room. The area was perhaps twelve feet by twenty, but scarce an inch of it was empty. Every surface, every nook and cranny and much of the floor space was piled high with an indescribable assortment of oddments that put even our Baker Street sitting-room to shame.

'My word, Holmes!' I whispered. 'This fellow is more of a magpie than you!'

He ignored my pleasantry and kept his eyes on our host, who was extracting from a dark corner of the hovel a bundle wrapped in oilskin. When he removed the oilskin I saw that it had covered a violin, but one that gleamed bright silver in the lamplight.

'Remarkable!' exclaimed Holmes. 'Would you be so good as to let us hear it, Mr Williams?'

The old man plucked the strings and quickly tuned his instrument, then picked up a bow and commenced to play. I enjoy a wide variety of music so long as it is well played, but I had nerved myself for a crude performance on an ill-sounding instrument. To my surprise our host extracted from his strange instrument a passably pleasant tone and his playing, though the melodies were only country dances and music-hall airs, exhibited no little skill.

Holmes removed a bundle of wire snares from a rickety kitchen chair and sat, apparently enthralled by the old man's performance. I pushed a pile of rabbit-skins aside and made myself comfortable on the top of an old tin trunk. Williams stood in the centre of the room, his bald head flung back and his eyes half closed. His greasy grey locks swung around his dark features as he worked at the instrument. I was so distracted by the music that I almost failed to notice when the left sleeve of his ragged shirt fell away from his forearm momentarily and revealed a glimpse of what was certainly the same tattoo that I had seen on the arm of the dead Lord Backwater.

I had no doubt that Holmes would have seen the mark, so I made no mention of it. The old man drew his recital to a close, opened his eyes and stared belligerently at Holmes.

'There y'are!' he exclaimed. 'What d'you say to that?'

'I say that is truly remarkable,' said Holmes. 'Tell me, Mr Williams, did you construct that instrument yourself?'

'Yes, I did,' said the fiddler. 'When I was... when I was at sea, I hadn't no wood to make one so I thought of tin and I put it together with tin-snips and solder.'

'It has a splendid tone,' said Holmes.

'Tidy enough,' said Williams, looking pleased. 'I finds a good rub down with a handful of sand puts a shine on her and makes her sound better.'

'May I try it?' asked Holmes, quickly adding when he saw a frown crossing the old man's features, 'I have a Stradivarius myself.'

'There's more than one Stradivarius,' said our host, 'but that's the only one as I ever made.' He handed Holmes the fiddle and bow. 'You'll find it difficult,' he said. 'She's back-strung.'

'I have exercised with both hands,' said Holmes and, after a few exploratory flourishes with the bow, he plunged into a spirited melody. Now it was the old man's turn to listen as Holmes ran through a medley of bright tunes.

At last he paused and enquired with seeming innocence, 'Did you ever hear this tune, Mr Williams?' and he launched into a sad, slow air.

The old man became visibly uneasy, but when Holmes lowered the bow he said, 'I can't say as I recall it, no.'

'Now you do surprise me,' said Holmes. 'I felt sure you would recognise it. Perhaps the words would help your memory.'

He cleared his throat and sang quietly but clearly:

'I've been a prisoner at Port Macquarie,
On Norfolk Island and at Emu Plains,
Upon Castle Hill and in cursed Toongabbie,
At all those settlements I've worked in chains,
But of all the places of condemnation,
The penal stations of New South Wales,
To Moreton Bay there must be no equal,
Excessive cruelty each day prevails.

'An exaggeration of the writer's, I believe,' he said, when his song was done. 'Surely Norfolk Island was worse than Moreton Bay?'

Williams' face had paled even under its coat of grime. 'Get out!' he snarled. 'You damned sneaking spies! Get out of my house!'

Holmes laid the gleaming violin and its bow carefully upon the corner of a cluttered table and looked the furious old man squarely in the eye.

'Whoever encouraged, paid or ordered you to the beech glade as a guide to those two killers has put a rope around your neck, Williams. I know that you did no more than that, but that may not save you from the gallows. Tell me what you know and I promise you I will save your neck.'

'Get out!' the old man roared again. 'I've nothing to say to the likes of you – not now and not never. Get out of my house!'

He lifted his gnarled fists threateningly.

'Very well,' said Sherlock Holmes calmly, 'but my offer remains open. Good-day to you, Williams, and thank you for the use of your instrument.'

We withdrew in good order and the makeshift door slammed at our backs with a volley of imprecations.

'Tell me,' I said to Holmes as we retraced our steps along the woodland path, 'how on earth did you know that Williams was left-handed?'

'When I observed the signs of a left-handed man in the beech glade,' he replied, 'we had just passed by the hedges of Colonel Caddage's estate and I had noted that his hedger was left-handed. It might not have been our man, but Inspector Scott's reference to a tin fiddle made me realise that Williams was not only left-handed but was possibly an old transport.'

This confused me even more. 'But how could you detect left-handedness from a hedge?' I asked.

'Very simply, Watson. A right-handed hedger takes a long shoot of the hedge in his left hand and bends it down. With a billhook in his right hand he then cuts the shoot part-way through just above the ground and weaves it into the hedgerow to his left to thicken and reinforce the hedge. A left-handed hedger must cut with the left hand and weave the shoots to his right.'

'But what has all this to do with Australia?' I asked.

We had come to a point where a gnarled root lay across our path and a drift of dead leaves was gathered behind it. I was in the act of stepping over the root when Holmes seized my shoulder in a steely grip and forced me to a halt.

'Step back, Watson!' he commanded.

I stepped cautiously backwards and watched as Holmes picked up a fallen branch and thrust it into the mass of dead leaves: there was a convulsion among the leaves and a sharp, metallic noise. Holmes lifted the branch and I could see that hanging from it was a rusted iron man-trap, its huge teeth firmly embedded in the wood.

'Great heavens!' I exclaimed. 'One of us might have been maimed! How did we miss that on the way here?'

'Very readily,' said Holmes, 'because it had not been put in place when we passed this way an hour ago.'

Six

A PAUSE FOR REFRESHMENT

'I stopped you,' continued Holmes, 'because I perceived that the drift of leaves behind that root had grown mysteriously deeper since we first came this way. Now,' he said, pointing with his stick, 'I see also a footprint familiar to me from the beech glade. At least one of Lord Backwater's murderers is still in the vicinity.'

'And close upon our trail!' I exclaimed.

'We are certainly observed,' he remarked.

'You sound pleased by the fact,' I said.

'Oh I am, Watson, I am. For if we draw the assassins' attention so greatly that they feel obliged to frighten us away, we cannot be very far wrong in our enquiries.'

I shuddered at the thought of the injury that rusty mantrap might have inflicted on Holmes or me and he eyed me sharply.

'Your narrow escape has shaken you, Watson. You must let me play the doctor this time and prescribe a pause for refreshment and a glass at the village inn.'

Once we had reached the road it was no great distance to the village, and a glass of brandy at the Backwater Arms soon bore out Holmes' prescription.

The little parlour was empty of customers and Holmes invited the landlord to drink with us, introducing us as guests at the forthcoming funeral.

'A sad business,' said the publican, 'that such a man as Lord Backwater should be so took.'

'He was well respected hereabouts?' said Holmes.

'Respected, sir, he was loved hereabouts. He was kindness itself to this village. Do you know he even paid for new tombstones for everyone as had people in the churchyard? You see when you goes to the funeral. Each could have whatever they wanted at his expense. A wonderful kindly man,' and he shook his head sadly.

'Tell me,' Holmes asked. 'Backwater Hall is a modern building but the estate is evidently an old one. Is there no Backwater Old Hall?'

'No, sir,' said the landlord. 'There was an old place as belonged to the Varleys. A ramshackle old place it were, hundreds of years old. When young Mr Varley disappeared, his dad let the place go, you know.'

'Disappeared?' queried Holmes.

'Oh yes, sir. He went to sea, young Varley, and he never come back and after some years he was presumed dead and his old father he just took to drink and let the whole place go to rack and ruin. Then he died and the old place was a-falling down. Lord Backwater bought it for a song. Of course he wasn't a Lord then, he was still Mr James Lisle.'

He drew at his cider and went on, 'First thing he did when he bought it was to burn it down.'

'Burn it down!' exclaimed Holmes, as though this was the first he had heard of it. 'How extraordinary!'

'Well, he did,' said our host, 'and he made a real do of it. He invited all the village and there was tables put out with food and I was to supply ale and cider and lemonade, all of which he paid for in advance. We had a rare old do, I can tell you, sir, singing and dancing and I don't know what.'

'Well, well,' said Holmes wonderingly. 'And what part did Lord Backwater play in the festivities?'

'He was here and there all the time, talking to everyone just as if it was me and you, sir. Then when it had all burned out and everyone was gone, me and my boys was loading the barrels and we seed him a-walking through the ashes.'

'Walking through the ashes!' I exclaimed.

'Oh yes, sir. I mind it to this day, how he walked through the hot ashes and he was all in his good clothes but he was kicking up the ash like a boy on a holiday. Then he stands in front and he gets down on his knees and it looked like he was saying a prayer. Very strange it seemed to me,' and he took a long, reflective draught of cider.

'I wonder,' said Holmes, 'if I might trouble you for a pen and paper. There is a message I must send while I am in the village.'

'No trouble at all, sir,' said our host and, reaching under his counter, he produced a pad of cheap writing-paper, a schoolroom pen and a crusted bottle of ink.

Holmes tipped the man and carried the items to a table by the window where, under the pretence of scribbling a note, he examined pen, ink and paper minutely. When he showed me the few lines he had scribbled I had no difficulty in agreeing with him that the message from the Gates of Hell had been written in this house.

He returned the writing materials to the landlord, ordered up more drinks and gazed reflectively out of the window.

'You are in a very pretty part of the country here,' he observed.

'We do think so, sir. It might not be entirely to our liking in winter, but this time of year the woods and hills is very pretty.'

'I've an acquaintance in London,' Holmes mused, 'who travels this area regularly on his business. He has often recommended it to me, but this is the first time I have found myself hereabouts. What is his name. Watson?'

My completely genuine inability to supply a name must have convinced the landlord.

'No, no use,' said Holmes. 'Neither of us can recall his name. You know him, Watson – tall fellow, a bit weathered about the face, talks with a colonial twang. What is his name?'

'Why,' said the landlord, 'that sounds like Mr Collins, Mr Peter Collins. He was here only days ago.'

'That's the man!' exclaimed Holmes. 'And I've missed him? What a great shame! Was he here long?'

'Oh no. He never stops long. Mr Collins comes every few months for just a night or two, never longer. I don't know his business, but I'd have thought it was connected with the sea.'

'I do believe that it is,' said Holmes. 'Tell me, was Mr Collins a friend of the late Lord Backwater? It would be extraordinary if Collins and I were both friends of his and never knew it.'

The landlord chuckled. 'No, sir, I think I can safely say that Mr Collins was not even an acquaintance of Lord Backwater. The first time as I had Mr Collins here he caused a bit of upset by speaking freely in the public bar, giving out radical opinions about the landed gentry. Now there's many hereabouts as received great kindness from Lord Backwater and they didn't care to hear that kind of thing, so I had to take him aside and explain that, being a publican, I has no politics but I should be grateful if he would draw it a bit mild. He was a perfect gentlemen about it, bought a round of drinks and never said another word out of place.'

'Well, well,' said Holmes, 'I would never have suspected Collins of radical opinions.'

'I hope you will not mention the matter to him,' said the landlord anxiously. 'I would not have him think as I had spoken out of turn.'

'Never fear, landlord,' replied Holmes. 'Like you I have no political opinions and the views of others may be what they wish.' He drew out his watch. 'I fear,' he said, 'that we have enjoyed your hospitality too long and must now return to Backwater Hall. Good-day, landlord.'

As we made our way out of the village I saw that my friend was smiling to himself, no doubt at the budget of fresh information that he had acquired from the garrulous landlord.

We had not gone far when a trap rounded a bend in the road ahead of us and I saw that it carried Inspector Scott.

'Mr Holmes, Dr Watson,' he hailed us. 'I have been looking for you. I gather you have visited Tin-Fiddle Williams.'

'Your intelligence service does you credit,' said Holmes as we climbed aboard. 'May I enquire how you knew?'

The police officer laughed. 'Because I had him in my office half an hour ago, accusing me of setting spies upon him and threatening to apply to the Chief Constable if I did not stop it.'

'Dear me,' said Holmes, 'we are rapidly wearing out our welcome in Backwater. The Chief Constable seeks any occasion to remove us from the county, our client is not convinced of my theories and now the village fiddler regards us as police spies. Nevertheless, Inspector, if your Chief Constable is even partly right and there is any poacher involved in Lord Backwater's death it is Williams.'

'Should I have him watched?' asked the Inspector.

'I would prefer it if you did not,' said Holmes. 'I have made him an offer which I think, upon reflection, he will find difficult to refuse.'

'What was that?' asked Scott.

'To tell me what he knows about Lord Backwater's death and to be saved from the gallows, or to remain silent and to hang with the perpetrators when I lay my hand upon them.'

'And do you believe that will work?' the Inspector enquired.

'I think it may,' said Holmes, 'and it would shorten my task, but I shall reach a conclusion with or without Williams' assistance.'

We had reached Backwater Hall. As we disembarked Holmes turned to the police officer. 'When next you report to Colonel Caddage,' he said, 'you may tell him that I was wrong in one respect. At our brief interview I told him that the roots of this matter lie a very long way away. That I still believe to be true but there is an aspect of the affair that has its origins here in Backwater.'

Seven

LORD BACKWATER'S WILL

Lord Backwater's funeral was to take place in the village on the following morning. Holmes wished to take particular account of those who attended and so we were at the church early.

It had been announced as a family funeral, but Lord Backwater's wealth and reputation, his kindness to the people of Backwater and the brutal manner of his death guaranteed that many more than family and friends would attend.

The station trap was busy all morning, delivering passengers to the little church, and the lane alongside the graveyard was filled with carriages in a short time, as there arrived from all over the country senior functionaries and, in many cases, aristocratic patrons of the charities that the late Viscount had supported. There were many widely known faces among the mourners and several senior coats of arms on the panels of the waiting carriages.

The tiny village church was too small to hold all of those who had come to pay their last respects and the villagers of Backwater gathered outside the porch. Prominent among the congregation we saw Colonel Caddage, which was predictable, but at the back of the gathering around the porch was Tin-Fiddle Williams, a degree less unclean than when we met him and apparently not anxious to advertise his presence.

I drew Holmes' attention to Williams, but he merely nodded.

'I had marked him,' he said, 'and I imagine that he is here because he dare not draw the villagers' attention by staying away. He is not who I had hoped to see.'

'You were, perhaps, expecting Collins or whatever his name is – the Man from the Gates of Hell?' I ventured.

'I had some slight hope that Mr Collins might make an appearance,' he replied. 'Still, the service has not begun, he may yet arrive.'

'But he was not a friend of Lord Backwater,' I said. 'The landlord told us how Collins spoke against the landed aristocracy.'

'A device, Watson,' said Holmes impatiently. 'A transparent ruse to convince the villagers that the cause that brought him to Backwater regularly was not to visit Lord Backwater. Whatever the nature of his business with the Viscount it was both secret and dangerous. I would remind you that the ambush in the beech glade was set for Collins, not for Lord Backwater.'

The last of the congregation seemed to have taken their places and I suggested to Holmes that we join them, but he wished to stay outside.

'I think the eulogies for Lord Backwater will be so predictable that they may be taken as read,' he remarked. 'There will be nothing to learn in the church but there may yet be data to be gleaned here.'

He strolled off across the churchyard and I followed. Our route brought us to the side of the cemetery where an open grave awaited Lord Backwater.

'It is not,' I remarked, 'a very prominent position for Backwater's most eminent citizen.'

'Exactly,' said my friend. 'It is, in fact, a rather obscure position for the village's most renowned resident.'

The waiting grave lay at the very edge of the churchyard, surrounded on three sides by existing burials. Holmes paced round the pit, looking at each of the inscriptions on the adjacent memorials.

'Watson,' he said, 'if you have your pocket-book, I wonder if you would be kind enough to write down these names for me.'

I took out my notebook and at his dictation recorded the following:

JOSEPH KEEP
cobbler of this village
1783 – 1847
also
ELISABETH KEEP
beloved wife of the above
1790 – 1845

FREDERICK JARMAN
1778 – 1852
Coachman to Squire Varley
for 51 years
Well done, thou good
and faithfull servant

PRUDENCE GROVER
Born 1835
Died in childbed 1852
Also John
an infant child
Born & died 1852

'Well,' I said when I had noted the epitaphs, 'these are humble companions in death for Britain's greatest philanthropist.'

'An elderly bachelor,' Holmes mused, 'an unmarried girl and a cobbler and his wife, and Lord Backwater will lie with the couple on his right, the old coachman at his left and the girl at his feet. You asked me once, Watson, what has Lord Backwater's murder to do with Australia. You might ask what it has to do with these graves.'

I had no opportunity to comment for at that moment the doors of the church opened and the Viscount's coffin was borne across the graveyard towards us.

Once the interment was over the villagers and many of the visitors left. Holmes kept a sharp eye on the departures and spoke briefly to our friend the landlord of the Backwater Arms, but there was still no sign of Peter Collins. The remainder of the mourners returned to Backwater Hall and Holmes and I accompanied them. At the funeral reception my friend's keen eyes still sought anyone who might be Collins, but without success.

When the guests had departed Lord Backwater invited us to join him and his sister in the library, where Mr Predge was about to read the deceased's will.

The solicitor laid out his papers carefully on the great library table, took out his spectacles and adjusted them, took a sip of water and then gazed around the table. Clearing his throat he began.

'Lord Backwater, Lady Patricia, gentlemen... I am sure that the principal provisions of the late Lord Backwater's will are straightforward and are well known to his heirs and it will, perhaps, suffice if I summarise them. There are, however, two less ordinary provisions and I shall come to these in a moment.'

He paused and gazed around him, but no one reacted to his announcement.

'Very well then. The entire estate of Lord Backwater, whether real or otherwise, with all investments, royalties and patents, descends intact to Lord Patrick apart from a list of bequests to local and national charities which are scheduled and certain personal bequests to existing and former retainers of the family. There is, of course, a provision, the details of which are known to Lord Patrick and Lady Patricia, to make allowance for Lady Patricia before and during any marriage and in the event of her widowhood or – ahem – the ending of any marriage. These arrangements are, as I have said, straightforward, and make Lord Patrick an extremely wealthy man and place Lady Patricia in a position of independence. The bequest to Lord Patrick is made subject to a hope that he will continue to support those charities that were always Lord Backwater's special concern, most particularly the support of the orphaned poor and victims of injustice.'

He paused again and Lord Backwater nodded as though to encourage him.

'I come now,' continued the solicitor, 'to two provisions which I am unable to explain inasmuch as Lord Backwater had them included in the testament without vouchsafing any reason to me.'

He drew a slip of paper from his document case and examined it for a moment before beginning to read from it.

'"I have provided my solicitor with details of the precise location at which I am to be interred and the necessary arrangements have been made with the incumbent of the village church, but I have not hitherto expressed any view as to the memorial to be placed on my grave. I now require and demand of my heir that there should be placed at the head of the grave a simple monument of the local stone bearing only the dates of my birth and death and the name..."'

'James Loveridge,' murmured Holmes.

The lawyer stopped, apparently dumb-struck, and all of us stared at Holmes in astonishment.

'May I ask how you knew that name, Mr Holmes?' enquired the solicitor.

'It is my business to know what others do not,' said Holmes, 'and my methods of discovering it are rarely unusual.'

'But my father's name was James Lisle!' exclaimed Lord Patrick. 'Why should he wish to be buried under a false name?'

Holmes remained silent and, after looking round the table again as though seeking an answer, Mr Predge continued.

'In addition to his requirement as to the memorial,' he said, 'Lord Backwater placed in my hands a document which, by the terms of the testament, I am obliged to hand, unopened, to his heir.' He took from his document case a bundle of papers, bound with lawyers' tape and heavily sealed. 'In the presence of witnesses I now do so,' he announced and passed the package to Lord Patrick. 'If Your Lordship will be good enough to observe that the seals are intact and are your father's.'

Lord Patrick turned the bundle in his hands. 'The seals are his,' he confirmed, 'and it bears a superscription in his hand – "For my son, Patrick". What is it, Predge?'

'I have no idea, Your Lordship. It was given to me by your father exactly as it is now. That was some six months ago and at the same time he altered his will so as to require that the packet be handed to you on his death. By doing so – and by making you aware of the other provisions of the will – I have, I hope, discharged my obligations in full.'

'I am sure you have, Predge,' said the young Lord. 'Now this looks as if it requires reading. If you will be kind enough to ring for the butler, Predge, I suggest that the rest of you take a little refreshment while I take this to my study and see if it throws any light upon my father's death.'

He stood up and Lady Patricia rose as well. 'I do not think I fancy any refreshment,' she said. 'If you will all excuse me I think I shall take a little fresh air in the park. I am sure that Patrick will let me know if there is anything of consequence to me in the document. Good afternoon, gentlemen.'

As Lord Backwater left us he turned in the doorway. 'Mr Holmes,' he said, with a half-smile, 'you have not told us how you knew the name that my father wished to be buried under. Do you, by any chance, know what this document contains?'

'I would be guessing if I were to claim so,' replied Holmes. 'While I can tell you the gist of it, and that it will go a long way towards solving the mystery of your father's death, I do not pretend to know the details. Nevertheless, I suspect you should be prepared for some startling revelations, Your Lordship.'

Eight

AN ORPHAN'S NARRATIVE

It was two hours before Lord Backwater returned to us, a thoughtful expression on his face. He held the unsealed bundle of papers in his hand.

When he had poured himself a large brandy he turned to us. 'Gentlemen,' he said, 'Mr Holmes was right on the two points he made. This document has startled me and it does, I believe throw some light on the death of my father. I believe you should all know what it contains. Perhaps you will excuse me if I do not read it to you, but I admit that a first reading of it has disturbed me. Predge, I wonder if you would be so kind?'

'Oh, of course, Lord Patrick,' said the little solicitor. Taking the document and adjusting his spectacles he began to read it. Through Lord Backwater's kindness in allowing me access to the manuscript at a later date, I am able to reproduce here the narrative exactly as we first heard it that afternoon:

My dear son, if this document comes into your hand it will be only because my death has prevented me from explaining to you matters which, perhaps, I should have laid bare much earlier. Certainly it is my intention, if I am spared and if certain plans are successful, to broach these matters with you in person but they are of such importance that I must not gamble against fate.

You will, by now, be aware that you are one of the wealthiest men in England, and I have no qualm in leaving in your hands the disposal of the vast sums that I was fortunate enough to accumulate. I know that you will conduct yourself as I would wish and that those whom I sought to assist will not suffer at your hands. However, you must know that among the many accounts which you now control is one which is not yours to dispense. It is held by Barings who are thoroughly reliable and you will find it identified in my ledgers as the "Black Queen" account. At the time of writing it stands at more than four-hundred-thousand pounds and you will see that many charitable donations have been drawn from it. Nevertheless, it was never mine and it is not yours. You must not draw upon that account unless and until the circumstances which I shall set out occur when there will be one at hand to instruct you as to the proper disposal of the funds.

To explain that embargo it is necessary for me to reveal a number of matters that may shock and distress you, but they are, nevertheless, matters that you have always had a right to know. If I have kept them from you it was because I would not burden you and later because the secret was not mine to reveal. Before my marriage I made a clean breast of these things to your mother, for it would have been wickedness to do otherwise. She accepted them with that calm that was her hallmark and agreed that they should lie between us alone until you were of age to share the burden.

What can I say of Joseph and Elisabeth Keep, the childless cobbler and his wife who gave us a home? Simple and humble folk though they were, they raised us to be honest and hardworking and gave us a childhood such as any man in England might envy. Their little cottage was always warm and clean, ripe with the scent of Aunt Lisa's cooking, and if we were not richly clad we were cleanly and decently dressed and well-shod by Uncle Joe's craft. Nor were our souls neglected, for as we grew we learned that our Aunt and Uncle expected nothing less than honesty, kindness and courage of us in all our dealings. A truthful admission of error would bring only a reprimand from Uncle Joe, but a lie would result in a strapping.

If I have done any good with my life it has been through the example of that gentle, Christian couple and it has always been my sorrow that their great kindness ended in tragedy and that I brought them, albeit innocently, to grief and to an early grave. When my years of wandering ended and I returned at last to Backwater I wept to see their unmarked graves. I could not do them honour without revealing my shadowed past and I hope that they will forgive the artifice by which I managed to raise a proper memorial to them.

Through ten years of my childhood I and my orphan friend were nurtured by Joseph and Elisabeth Keep, growing in those years to be as much to each other as any brothers. The woods and fields were our playground in all seasons, even the Squire's lands were open to us as the result of an incident which, though of no great matter at the time, was to end our happiness and the lives of our good foster-parents.

My foster-brother, perhaps because he came of a tribe of acrobats and tumblers, grew into an active, sporting boy who outpaced the village boys in running, swimming and many other activities. He was no less able with his fists and grassed much older boys in bouts fair and otherwise and he had that Irish temperament that will neither be put upon itself nor see another ill used. In our days at the village school no child needed to fear the attentions of a schoolyard bully, for my friend's fists were always at the disposal of those less able than himself.

Squire Varley's only heir was a boy of my friend's years, though nowhere near so robust. Rupert Varley was a slight youth whose appearances around the village provoked jeers from the rougher element among the local boys. On one occasion my companion and I surprised a group of such youths who were making their cruel sport of young Varley. With a very little assistance from me, my friend delivered them such a drubbing as they would not soon forget and sent them on their ways.

Whether from genuine admiration and gratitude or merely from a sense of self-preservation, after this episode the Varley boy attached himself to us at every opportunity. This might have been an embarrassment had he not proved fully willing to join us in those forbidden activities of boyhood such as poaching and scrumping. In the event, as I have said, the companionship of the Varley boy opened to us the whole of his father's lands with but one exception.

Backwater Manor Farm was kept in those days by a man named Wells, a surly individual who bore a bad name in the district for his hard usage of his labourers and servants and his rude and crafty dealings with the world at large. My foster-brother and I had long ago determined to give his land a wide berth, having been many times warned off it with threats and curses. Rupert Varley was always attempting to lead us on to Wells' property by way, I believe, of establishing that the Squire's son could not be gainsaid. That might have been true, but we commoners did not care to chance Wells' anger.

There came a day, in the summer of 1842, when our landed companion was home from his school but was not accompanying my foster-brother and me. I cannot recall now how we passed that day, presumably in the usual aimless pursuits of country boyhood. There was then no reason to mark the day and since then the recollection has been deeply overlaid. Had we known that it was to be the last day of our carefree youth we should have paid more mind.

We returned home from our pastimes in the late afternoon. As we entered our foster-parents' little cottage we saw Mr Stanley, the parish constable, seated at the table. Uncle Joe sat in his chair, his face grim and pale, and Aunt Lisa hovered between, her eyes red.

'Well, at last,' said Mr Stanley, and rose from his seat. 'I am afraid', he said to our foster-parents, 'that these two must go with me to the lock-up.'

We were dumbfounded. For once we knew of no offence of ours, large or small, that had gone undiscovered, but the constable soon threw us into further confusion and great fear.

'Come, my lads,' he said. 'I must take you into custody on suspicion of the unlawful firing of a rick of hay.'

Behind us as he shepherded us out Aunt Lisa wailed helplessly.

Nine

VICTIMS OF THE SYSTEM

The horror that seized our young minds when we learned that we had been taken up on suspicion of a capital offence was beyond imagining. Every child throughout the West knew the dreadful stories of the fate of the rick-burners of ten years ago, how few had hanged but the Special Commission that sat at Winchester had transported hundreds to Van Diemen's Land, never to see their homes and their loved ones again.

In that summer of '42 the mining and manufacturing districts were in a state of unrest. The Militia were out in the Midland counties against the coal and iron-workers. In the Western counties the authorities believed that the poor labourers had been so cowed by the fate of the Winchester transports that the region would remain quiet, but some suspicious magistrates rode the lanes day and night with their constables, seeking any sign of disaffection.

Constable Stanley lodged us in his lock-up and would tell us nothing of the reasons why we were taken in. His good wife, who had ever before been a friend to us, fed us and wept each time she saw us, calling us 'poor doomed orphans' and praying aloud for us, which did little to calm our fears.

It was not many days before we were brought before three of the magistrates for the division, one of whom was Squire Varley. He had always treated us in a distant but kindly enough fashion and we looked for nothing but fair play at his hands. Constable Stanley had explained, to us that we should now hear the evidence against us and that the Squire and his colleagues would decide whether a case had been made out against us, so that we were both fearful of the proceedings but also hopeful that our ordeal would soon end when the truth was heard.

Farmer Wells was called to the Book and sworn. As I have said, he was a man who owed nobody goodwill, and he soon set out a tale of our incursions upon his land and the many times he had driven us off. In answer to a question from a Justice he was honest enough to admit that he had not seen us on his property in nearly two years, but suggested that as we grew older we had grown craftier and less easy to spot.

He told of conversations in the village inn that seemed to him to be treasonable, and of his fears that the industrial unrest would spread to the countryside and barns and ricks would burn as they had ten years before, and finally he told how, on the day we were taken up, he had been told by Rupert Varley that his big rick in Backwater Bottom was afire. He had hastened there with his men, but the fire had got too good a hold and most of the stack had been destroyed.

Now I know that much of Farmer Wells' testimony should not have been heard, but neither the Justices nor their clerk made any move to stop him. Had we but a lawyer at our side short work might have been made of his story. True, when the clerk told Uncle Joseph that he might question the farmer on our behalf, Wells acknowledged that he had never seen us on the day in question and that he did not know, of his own knowledge, how his rick came to be fired or by whom.

This answer heartened us and we were further cheered when the next witness was sworn, for it was Rupert Varley. He owed us fair play and knew how we had long avoided the Manor Farm and now we expected to hear our innocence established.

We were cruelly disappointed, for Rupert Varley took his oath that my friend and I had sworn vengeance on the farmer after being driven off his lands. I can see him still, standing as innocent as an angel before his father's approving eye. They say that those who know the truth can smile at lies, but we could not smile as that wretched boy spilled out his lies. He told how we had asked him to join us among the ricks to smoke a pipe of tobacco, that he had not been willing but was afraid of my foster-brother. So he had gone to join us, but late, and on his way there had seen us both, daubed with smoke and fleeing from the rick which was then beginning to burn. He had run straight away for Farmer Wells in hope that the rick might be saved.

Uncle Joseph questioned the liar in vain; Rupert stood by his falsehoods in every particular and left the witness box with the thanks of the Justices for his part in the affair.

Constable Stanley was the last witness, and it must be said that he spoke only the truth of how he had come to arrest us, going so far as to remark that neither of us nor our clothing bore any mark or smell of smoke when we had come home. Even so the clerk interrupted him to ask if we might not have cleaned ourselves in some stream or pool before returning and the constable had to say that we could have done so. The Justices nodded at that and our hearts sank.

So all the case against us was the farmer's ill-will and Rupert's lies, but it took Their Worships little time to decide that we should stand trial and we were taken away to the county gaol.

If we had been miserable in Constable Stanley's lockup we thought we had now descended to the lowest pit of Hell. Chained at the ankles we were flung into a common cell of forty or so prisoners. Many of our nights passed sleeplessly, with me huddled in my foster-brother's arms weeping from terror of the future and him roundly cursing Rupert Varley for his treachery.

As the weeks passed we grew ever more like the wan and tattered creatures around us and ever less hopeful of our case. God bless our Aunt and Uncle that never a week passed but they made the long journey from Backwater on the carrier's cart, to bring us hope and encouragement and small gifts of food and goods that eased our hardships a little. On one such visit, when Aunt Lisa was unwell and Uncle Joe came alone, he confided to us that he was contemplating the sale of his little shop to provide funds for a lawyer when we came to the Assize, but we both told him that he must not do it. So much sorrow had come from his kindness to us that we could not see him lose his livelihood over us.

'But a lawyer might make all the difference,' he said. 'And he might not if Rupert Varley clings to his lies,' said my foster-brother, 'and if he does, we shall hang and you would be mourning us in the workhouse. No, Uncle, you must not.'

Our trial came up in the winter and on a cold, dull day we were taken to the Assize Hall. We had by then been months in gaol and wretched specimens we must have seemed, though our dear foster-parents brought us new clothes that we might not stand before our Judges in the rags we wore in gaol.

Our Aunt and Uncle tried to inspire us with hope of release, but we had lain too long among those who had experience of the courts. We had none to speak for us and we should not be allowed to speak for ourselves. Both of us knew in our hearts that, if the tale was told as it had been before the Justices, our only hope lay in being transported and not hanged.

Our trial done we waited hopelessly for the verdict. All had proceeded as in the lower court and again we had no lawyer to speak for us and could not speak for ourselves.

At last the jury returned their verdicts of guilty upon us both and now all that was left was to know if we were to live in misery or die.

The Judge looked down on us from beneath the painted and gilded arms of England and I was sure he was for hanging us. I recall little of his words, but I shall never forget his face. As he came to pronounce sentence on us his eyes glittered and he wet his lips. I have seen that look often since, in the faces of those who are about to order the death of a man or the flogging of a child or the chaining of a woman, and I do not doubt that the evil that lit that Judge's eyes shines in the eyes of all who punish misfortune and innocence, whether gaolers, Judges or Ministers of the Crown.

'So it is ordered and adjudged by this court that each of you be transported upon the seas, beyond the seas, to such place or places as Her Majesty, by the advice of her Privy Council, shall think fit to direct and appoint, for the term of fourteen years. Take them down,' he commanded, and we were hauled below and fettered to the wall to await the cart that would take us to the hulks.

We lay, most of that winter, in a rotten old hulk upon the mudbanks by Portsmouth, and even there our faithful Aunt and Uncle came to us as often as they might. There, too, we sank into a lower circle of "the System", being now convicted and confined among others awaiting transportation.

At length a rumour passed among us that we were to be part of a ship-load of boys loading for Port Arthur in Van Diemen's Land. For all we knew or understood of our destination we might as well have been bound for the moon. All we could hear of it from our fellow prisoners was that it was called "the Gates of Hell".

Ten

To The Gates Of Hell

On a dreary March day, with rain shrouding the land, we were taken from the hulk and sent aboard the transport *Henrietta*. Hardly were we below decks and the gratings closed above us than we heard the rattle of her anchor chains and felt the *Henrietta* move out into the Channel. So we were deprived of even a farewell glimpse of our native land, let alone a farewell to our loved ones. We were well away from land before the gratings were raised and our ankle-irons struck off.

How long our journey to the Gates of Hell took I can only surmise. I imagine we were some four months on the voyage but to a child (and I was no more) time is endless. We had, whatever the case, ample time to weigh up our fellow travellers.

We were boys of all ages from nine years to eighteen, but mostly of one kind. The greater part of us were out of the slums of London and the manufacturing towns of Lancashire and Staffordshire, gutter arabs steeped in the petty villainy of their kind, but few so wicked as to have merited the punishment to which we were being sent. There were indeed some older boys who were hardened to crime and these soon set themselves apart as petty chieftains within our society, preying upon and demanding subservience of their less violent fellows, their operations being ignored by the overseers. The minority of country boys in our number were easy prey for these bullies but the ready and able fists of my foster-brother kept us free of them.

With the *Henrietta*'s crew we had little to do. They were merely working seamen who had a cargo to ship from Portsmouth to Port Arthur, caring no more whether we were boys or sacks of grain, and they left us to the tender mercies of our guards. Those who guarded us were, like ourselves, a mixture. Some were not beyond a kind word or gesture, but others were beasts, who took our status as a licence to visit on us every kind of cruel whim. Barely had our first night at sea begun when some of them were amongst us, dragging away small boys for a purpose which I did not then understand but as to which my fellow travellers soon enlightened me. This became a nightly practice and those boys who were chosen and resisted were beaten until they succumbed. Still other boys were so steeped in depravity they offered themselves in return for favours, but even the lowest of the street arabs spoke of these with scorn, calling them 'hoofs'.

As day after weary day followed at sea the younger children wept for their lost homes, some of the older boys bragged of their hardness and how well they would survive in Van Diemen's Land, while others spoke endlessly of escaping.

To where might we have escaped? We knew nothing of our whereabouts save that we were somewhere on the ocean, battened under gratings except during our brief exercises on deck. My foster-brother warned me to put no hope in escape, not, at the least, until we were landed.

One bright spot in that long, miserable voyage was the 'Crossing of the Line'. On that day we were allowed on deck to join the crew in their celebrations and for a short hour or two could almost forget who we were and where we were bound, being briefly children again involved in the comic antics of the sailors.

Not long after, we touched land at Rio de Janeiro, though we did not know our whereabouts at the time. Here the *Henrietta* lay for some days to replenish her supplies. The first night in harbour we lay in the stifling heat and reek of our pens below decks while warm air seeped through the gratings, laden with the smell of grass and trees and fruit. On the next afternoon we were allowed on deck and straight away one of our number sprang into the shrouds and leaped into the water. He had made only a few strokes towards the shore when a musket banged and he sank.

The rest of us were driven below and the hatches replaced. While we remained in port all our guards went armed and we were not permitted on deck but lay, day and night, in sweating misery and gloom, tantalised by the smell of land.

I learned later from one of the *Henrietta*'s crew that our poor friend's corpse was not even recovered from the water, but left to wash like flotsam in the tide of a harbour whose very name he never knew.

At last, however, this portion of our ordeal ended. Though we had not been allowed on deck to see the last of England we were permitted to witness the *Henrietta*'s arrival at Cape Raoul. As we filed on deck some of our number cheered to see land so close, but that little enthusiasm died away with a second look.

The coast that faced us was of towering black cliffs, wreathed in mist. The rock was formed in fantastic flutes that reared up out of a roaring, boiling sea whose spray created the mist. Nowhere else in my travels across the world have I ever seen so formidable a shore.

Before our vessel turned the entrance into Port Arthur we could see that identical black cliffs formed the other side of the gateway and there must have been in all our minds the memory of that dread soubriquet: The Gates of Hell.

Once the ship had anchored in Port Arthur we were soon ironed by pairs at the ankle and sent ashore. There we were handed over to the colony's own guards and marched to our destination, the boys' reformatory at Point Puer.

As Port Arthur lies on a peninsula almost separated from the body of Van Diemen's Land, so Point Puer is a small promontory separate from the men's barracks at Port Arthur. The land in the area is much covered by fern and gum forest, but on Point Puer little grows for it has no water. If our hearts had sunk at the sight of the Gates of Hell, now they sank farther at the view of this barren area, clothed only with the buildings of the reformatory and surrounded mostly by cliffs as grim as those at Cape Raoul.

Before our irons had been removed we were paraded before the Commandant, who spoke to us at length, explaining that we should be taught useful trades here and that, if we were amenable to discipline, we should leave Point Puer better than we had come, but we listened with only a part of our attention for each of us was looking down the long vista of the years that we must spend there.

All, perhaps, except my foster-brother. When at last we had the chance of speech in the dormitory to which we were assigned he rallied me with, 'Cheer up, Jim. We are on dry land and can begin to think of a way out. From now on we must learn all we can about this place and how it works.' I had learned through all my short life to trust in him and in the crushing darkness of that first night at Point Puer his words were a little candle to me.

On the next day all of us new arrivals were marched some miles to a place called Eaglehawk Neck. This was the only way out by land, a long strip of hummocky grassland some one hundred yards wide from sea to sea. We had been taken there to see the futility of any attempt at escape. Stationed on the Neck were twenty-five armed guards but they were largely unnecessary for the way across was closed by a stout fence. On each post of the fence hung a great lantern and beneath each lantern was set a barrel in which was chained a ferocious dog. All the area in front of the fence was cleared of grass and covered in crushed white sea shells, the better to reflect the lanterns' lights at night. At each end of the fence it was carried out on to platforms over the sea, still within reach of the chained dogs.

That night I was less disposed to believe in my foster-brother's plan. 'There is no way across the Neck,' I whispered. 'There is,' he replied firmly, 'and we shall take it.'

Now we were introduced to the daily duty of Point Puer. Each morning we rose at five o'clock, wrapped up our hammocks and assembled for prayers and Bible readings until seven, when we broke our fast. After food, we washed and were inspected, then sent to our classes until noon when we washed again for inspection. At half-past five we were given our last meal and at a quarter-after-six we assembled for two hours of school lessons before we turned in. In between times we were all available to the guards as cleaners, carriers, messengers and general purpose labourers to our own camp and the men's barracks.

The classes we attended were meant to fit us for an honest trade when our sentence was done, classes in carpentry, blacksmithing, building and bootmaking. This last class attracted my foster-brother and me because of the slight skills we had learned in Uncle Joseph's little workshop and we became tolerably good bootmakers.

Each night we fell exhausted into our hammocks, yet still my foster-brother found the energy at every spare moment to exercise those athletic skills that had been his pleasure at home, urging me to do the same.

I did not sleep so soundly that I was unaware of activity in the dormitory at night. The vileness that had haunted our nights at sea still went on, but I became aware of something else. Each dormitory at night was watched by an overseer – the 'night cocky' as we called him – and no boy was supposed to leave the room until the morning bell. Nevertheless there were nights when as many as a dozen of the older boys left accompanied by the overseer, who would threaten the rest of us to make no disturbance nor to leave the room. I never stayed awake long enough to know when they returned, but the next morning would find them all in their hammocks and the overseer at his place. I asked my foster-brother if he knew what was taking place but he told me only to 'wait and see'.

On one such night I was watching covertly from my hammock when he slid out of his hammock above and shook me. 'Come with me!' he commanded, so I followed him and the others. A group of more than a dozen of us trooped silently after the overseer up to a higher floor where he unlocked the door of a store-room.

Inside he set his candle on the bare floor and all of us squatted around it. Looking at the circle of half-naked youths in the candlelight I saw that this was no prank; their faces were all fixed in earnest expressions and most were looking at me and my foster-brother.

Now the overseer counted those present and spoke to us. 'We are here gathered,' he said, 'to make two new Brothers,' and he indicated my foster-brother and me.

'Give them the oath!' he commanded, and the whole circle joined hands and chanted in unison.

'Hand in hand,
On earth or in Hell,
Sick or well,
On sea or land,
On the square, ever!

Stiff or in breath,
Lagged or free,
You and me,
In life or death,
On the cross, never!

The last line of each verse was shouted vigorously and, when it was done, my foster-brother and I were commanded to repeat it from memory. After each attempt the group repeated their performance until we could chant it perfectly. Then we were commanded to hold out our arms.

Immediately we were seized by two boys each and I flinched as something scored the flesh of my forearm but my guards held me firmly. Soon I realised that a pattern was being scratched upon my flesh and, once the initial pain was past, became more interested in working out what was being marked on me. I could not do so until the work was complete, the blood wiped away and a dark substance had been rubbed into the wounds. Then I could see that one arm bore a square with the word 'EVER' written within and the other a cross with the word 'NEVER' inscribed upon it. I knew that they were to serve as a warning and a reminder of the oath that I had sworn.

'Now, my friends,' said the overseer when both of us had been tattooed, 'you are both Brothers of the Ring,' and the circle round us cheered.

Eleven

BROTHERS OF THE RING

I remained totally bewildered by the ritual through which I had just passed, but I was soon enlightened. Our erstwhile overseer, now apparently the master of this bizarre Lodge, outlined to us the duties and rights permitted to membership of the Ring.

The Ring, it seemed, was a secret association of convicts and guards, bound under their oath to act always 'on the square' towards a Brother and never to be 'on the cross' with one – that is to act or speak against him. We must assist a Brother in all things and conceal a Brother's secrets. The sanctions behind the oath were two-fold, maiming in a seeming 'accident' for minor incursions, death for anything greater, either at the hands of the Brotherhood or by being informed against for another's capital crime.

My blood ran cold at his recital, which was so fiercely made it could not be disbelieved. In the scant time I had been at Port Arthur I knew of a number of boys who had been injured or killed in accidents in the timber-gangs, the building works or the smithy and now I did not doubt that some of these had been the Ring's work.

Our overseer then pronounced the formal business of the meeting ended and produced a bottle of rum which was soon circulating from hand to hand or rather from mouth to mouth.

I had never tasted spirits before and the effect of the rum on me was to quench all my doubts and fears about this strange Brotherhood of which I now made one. Soon I was as merry as any in the company, while we sang songs that some of the older boys had brought with them from the mainland of Australia. Ordinarily these were known as 'treason songs' and the singing of even a snatch of one merited flogging, but now we sang them at length in chorus. There was 'Jim Jones':

> *By night and day the irons clang and like poor galley slaves,*
> *We toil and at our end must fill dishonoured graves,*
> *But by and by I'll break my chains, into the bush I'll go,*
> *And join the bold bushrangers there, Jack Donahue and Co.*

> *And some dark night when everyone is sleeping in the town,*
> *I'll kill the tyrants one and all and shoot the floggers down,*
> *I'll give them all a little shock, remember what I say,*
> *They'll yet regret they sent Jim Jones in chains to Botany Bay.*

And there was the song of Donahue himself:

> *As Donahue was riding out one summer's afternoon,*
> *He had no notion that his death was drawing in so soon,*
> *A Sergeant of the Horse Police discharged his carabine,*
> *And called aloud on Donahue to fight or to resign,*
> *Resign to you, you cowardly scum, is a thing I shall not do,*
> *But I'll fight this night with all my might! Cried bold Jack*
> *Donahue.*

He fought six rounds with the Horse Police until that fatal ball,
Which pierced his heart and made him start,
caused Donahue to fall,
And as he closed his mournful eyes and bade this world adieu,
He said, Convicts all, both large and small, say prayers for
Donahue.

We sang through many such until the candle guttered low and it was time to slip back to our hammocks.

Next morning I suffered the effects of coarse spirits on the inexperienced, but even so, there returned to my mind the questions that had perplexed me at the Ring's meeting. If there was something worse than the official cruelty of the System it must surely be this secret Brotherhood of guards and convicts, sworn on their lives to turn their hands against any man except a Brother.

At our first private moment I questioned my foster-brother why he had led us into such a group.

'You know Hunter, that beastly over-seer?' he asked.

'Of course,' I said, for the man was a byword for his drunkenness, brutality and loathsome vice. 'What of him?'

'He has set his eye upon you,' said my companion.

'He has asked others if you are not a hoof. He is a Brother himself and now he must not turn his hand against you.'

My blood froze at the thought of the danger that had threatened me. 'But is this Ring not a gang of cut-throats?' I asked.

'So they may be,' he replied, 'but they have power, and we need their help if we are to escape from here.'

'When will that be?' I implored him fervently.

'Soon enough,' he said, 'when all my plans are ripe.'

He did not take me into his plans, believing, no doubt, that I was protected by not knowing, but now I chafed through each weary, toilsome day wondering when we should make our attempt.

Some weeks passed uneventfully and then we found that the vile Hunter was assigned amongst the overseers of our dormitory. I took little regard of it at first, believing that my membership of the Ring would protect me, but it was not to be.

The first night he had the duty he summoned me to his table when all the dormitory was asleep.

'Now,' he said, 'they tell me you are a Brother. Show me the marks of a Brother!'

I put forward my arms to expose the tattoos and he examined them. 'Well,' he said, 'it seems you are, so you must know that we Brothers must always do each other's bidding,' and there was that look in his bloated features that I had seen on the Judge's face.

'I swore an oath to help my Brothers and to keep their secrets, not to do all that they wished,' I said, with as much firmness as I could muster, for this bloated, red-faced man terrified me.

'Then you shall learn what happens to those who will not obey a Brother,' he hissed and, seizing me by the neck, flung me face down across his table.

I had scarcely landed on the table before the first blow of the overseer's cane stung me across my naked shoulders. Even in my extremity of fear and pain I could not cry out, for if my foster-brother woke he would surely kill Hunter.

So I lay silent under his onslaught while he thrashed my back to ribbons. When his rage had abated he dragged me back to my hammock and flung me to the floor beneath it. I could not climb into the hammock, but dragged down my blanket and spread it on the floor. There, on a blanket stiffened by my own blood, my foster-brother found me at the five o'clock bell. As I had believed, he was for killing Hunter and paying the price, but I persuaded him to defer to the discipline of the Ring.

This was done, but gave us little satisfaction, for Hunter claimed I had been grossly insubordinate within the earshot of others and that he had been forced to punish me. I understood then that I must submit to Hunter or get away, and from that day on I pressed my foster-brother to complete his arrangements for our escape.

The wounds of Hunter's violence had scarcely healed when there came another night when he called me to his table. He leered at me under the watch-lantern and said, 'Have you now learned your lesson, Brother?'

I feared that another such beating would be the end of me, but I stood firm and answered him, 'I should die rather than submit to you!'

'Then so you shall!' he snarled, and sprang at me with his cane. The agony of the blows he inflicted was greater than before, cutting as they did across my half-healed injuries, but suddenly the attack ceased and I heard Hunter make a strange grunting noise.

A pair of hands lifted me from the table and I saw a ring of boys about me. Hunter lay on the floor in a pool of blood and over him stood my foster-brother, still holding the stool with which he had struck him down.

Jemmy the Pick, a locksmith's apprentice from Brummagem, stepped forward and bent over Hunter. When he looked up his face was white in the lantern-light.

'Glory be, cully!' he exclaimed. 'You've killed the swine!'

My foster-brother's face never altered, but he turned to me. 'Can you run, Jim?' he asked. 'We must be across the Neck while it is still well dark.'

With Hunter's keys we opened the store-room on the floor above and there we changed into civilian clothing which had been concealed there by the Ring. Before leaving the barracks we returned to the dormitory, where my foster-brother dabbled our uniform trousers and shirts in Hunter's blood and crammed them in a flour-sack which he brought with us.

Jemmy escorted us to the barracks door. 'How will you do?' asked my foster-brother.

'We shall blame it all on you,' said Jemmy. 'We shall say we was all asleep until it was over and we woke to find Hunter down and you two bolted. They ain't gonna take us all to Sydney for trial. It's you as needs to worry. If the puppies or the sharks don't get you, they'll hang the pair of you.'

And with that grim farewell we set out to escape from Point Puer.

Twelve

ACROSS THE NECK

A cold wind whipped across Eaglehawk Neck, whistling in the long, coarse grass and chilling the sweat on our faces. We had run and jogged from Point Puer in good time and now lay hidden in the long grass towards the southern limit of the fence.

'Where are the guards?' I asked my foster-brother.

'Inside their bungalows,' he replied. 'They rely on the dogs. Until they hear the dogs make a noise they have no need to stir outside. If word had reached them that we were out they would be ready for us.'

'How will we cross the fence?' I asked.

'You,' he said, 'will go down to the beach and walk along the water's edge, but keep your eye on me. Now, you see the curves where the dogs' feet have marked?'

I looked, and on the lamplit area of white shells I could see where each dog had marked out the circular limit of its chain.

'You will see me walk out between the last two curves and put this down.' He reached in the flour-sack and drew out a chunk of raw meat. 'The last dog on land will go for it and the second one will try for it as well. As soon as you see me put the meat down, run along the waterline to the platform and throw this to the platform dog,' and he passed me a chunk of meat. 'Throw it as far along the platform as you can. Then, when the platform dog is after the meat and the land dogs are fighting, go fast over the end of the fence. Right at the end – as far as you can get from the dogs.'

'What will you do?' I asked.

'Once the dogs start a noise the guards will soon be here. As soon as you're across I shall run for the end of the fence, as far as I can get from the last land dog and the platform dog, and climb over. Now, there's one last thing, when you get down to the sea, throw these in the water,' and he handed me my blood-dabbled convict clothing. 'With any luck they may find them and think the sharks got us. I'll drop mine further along when I've crossed the fence. Now, have you got it all?'

I nodded dumbly. 'Let's go, then,' he said. 'Good luck, Jim!'

I wished him the same and slid off through the grass towards the beach. The tide was well up and I was soon walking along the water's edge. Dropping the bundle of clothing into the sea I watched for my foster-brother's move.

At last I saw him dash out from the long grass and place his bait before hiding again. In a very short time, the underfed dogs caught the smell of the meat and came out to investigate. I quickened my pace and trembled as the platform dog slouched out of its barrel, rattling its long chain.

When I judged it time I lobbed my meat as far down the platform as I could and watched thankfully as the black shape of the dog moved off towards it. I dared not wait a second, but now ran to the fence and scrambled up it, dropping thankfully to the sand on the other side.

'Come on!' I called, as loudly as I dared, for the two land dogs were now snarling noisily over the meat and I feared the arrival of the guards. Suddenly he sprang out of the shadows beyond the white shells and sprinted for the fence.

I knew his speed and had no doubt that he would be well up the fence before the nearest dog could reach him. I was silently cheering him on when disaster struck. I do not know if his ankle turned or if he lost his footing on the shells and pebbles, but suddenly he was sprawling on the ground.

I watched in horror as he started to struggle to his feet, only to be dragged down by the end dog. They fought on the ground and I saw him desperately trying to entangle the animal in its chain, but its weight and ferocity were too much for him. Maddened by the smell of blood on his clothing, it tore fiercely at him. I saw it lunge at his throat and heard his ringing cry as it struck. Then he lay still and I saw blood spreading on the white shells.

I might have clung to the fence for ever, but I heard voices coming and some instinct of preservation sent me running into the darkness. How long or how far I ran that night I do not know. I stumbled through the bush, reckless of pursuit, sobbing aloud, until exhaustion stopped me and I crawled into the branches of a tree to rest.

The sun was high when I woke. The memory of the night's events returned and filled me with grief and fear, bringing fresh tears to my eyes. In my despair I contemplated flinging myself into the sea and ending my misery, but the knowledge that my brave companion had made his sacrifice so that I should be free prevented me.

I knew that Port Arthur could signal an escape to the guards on the Neck in a minute and to Hobart in an hour, and I expected at every moment to hear the pursuit, but I also knew that I must move. My foster-brother had told me that we could find Hobart by keeping the sea always on our left and moving south and with only those directions I set out.

The miles from Port Arthur to Hobart are such as a sturdy boy might walk with ease in three or four days, but that is by the roads and I did not dare to travel by road. Stumbling through bush and gum forest I took far longer. There in the southern hemisphere the stars were unknown to me, but I knew that the sun's positions at dawn and sunset were not reversed and, by that and by keeping close to the coast, I made my way.

At Port Arthur the guards had discouraged us from escaping by telling us tales of escapers who had been eaten by the native blacks and of Pearce who escaped with a party from Macquarie Harbour and killed and ate his companions when they were starving. Raised in the country, I was able to feed myself off the land as I went, though not well. Each night I spent exhausted and still hungry in the branches of a tree, recalling the guards' stories of bolters who had been bitten by poisonous snakes or eaten by tigers.

One night I woke in my uncomfortable perch to hear an animal snuffing about the base of the tree. Beneath me I could see a large, dog-like creature with striped flanks staring up at me. I do not know what it was, but I froze with terror and dared not sleep again for fear of dropping into its maw. It prowled the area for the rest of the night, only abandoning its patrol when dawn broke.

After how many days I do not know I found myself on the banks of a stream so large I believed it to be the Derwent and began to follow it down to the port of Hobart. My clothes were now ragged and stained with my long struggle through the bush, and I knew that I dared not appear in the port as a ragamuffin, but now I was coming across occasional farms and from one I was able to steal myself a new outfit without being detected.

So I found my way at last to Hobart and, having learned to survive in the wild, had now to learn how to survive in the town. Apart from soldiers, who were everywhere in evidence, the port was also patrolled by a convict police force and both bent their efforts to taking up anyone who might be an assigned convict misbehaving or a runaway. In those days there were still few settlers in the island and boys on their own were rare.

I loitered about the wharves and jetties as much as I dared, my ears always alert for word of the sailing of an American ship, for I knew no English vessel would take me. Sometimes I helped the wharfies at their labour for a few pennies, telling them that I was the son of a settler on the far edge of Hobart. I found myself a hiding-place in an old barrel under a wharf, surrounded by rotting crates and debris. There I passed my nights, living on the wharfies' pence and what food I could scrounge or steal.

At last I saw a Yankee schooner lying in the harbour, the *Sarah Jane*. I watched her skipper coming and going ashore as the vessel unloaded and I wondered how long she would stay before a cargo was found for America. I grew more determined daily that the ship would not leave Hobart without me, but I knew that outbound vessels were searched by the convict police and heavy fines imposed on the master and crew of a ship that carried a runaway.

I was huddled in my barrel one night, musing on this problem, when I heard voices close at hand. I feared discovery and any attendant inquisition, but the sounds came no nearer to my hiding-place.

As I lay in the dark and listened I distinguished the voices of three men and could make out much of what they were saying. I listened with particular attention when I heard one of them mention the *Sarah Jane*. To my horror I realised that these were thieves. Somehow they had learned that the captain of the *Sarah Jane* would be paid for his delivered cargo on the following day and they proposed to waylay him on the foreshore and rob him before he returned aboard.

Their conference ended and I lay in my barrel, both frightened and elated. Fate had given me the opportunity to be of service to the Yankee schooner's master if I had the courage to take the risk.

Next morning the captain came ashore as usual and I saw him stride away into the town. I dared not leave the wharf all day lest I miss his return. At last, in the late afternoon, a carriage came along the wharf and stopped to let the captain out. He shook hands with the occupant of the carriage and strode to the wooden steps that led down to the foreshore. Anxiously I looked around for a sign of the robbers but saw none.

The Yankee skipper had reached the foreshore and signalled for his crew to send a boat when I saw three men slip from under the wharf and advance noiselessly on his back.

I flung myself down the wooden steps, calling out, 'Captain! Captain! Behind you!'

He turned and, seeing the thieves advancing on him, groped in his pocket for a weapon. Beyond him I saw his ship's boat on the water, but it would never reach the shore in time to prevent robbery and perhaps murder. As the three villains closed with the American I raced down the beach and flung myself on their rear.

The attackers were all large, muscular men, two of whom I had seen working on the wharves, and they were armed with blackjacks, but the American put up a stout defence, laying about him vigorously. My assistance was but little, though I attacked as fiercely as I was able and I believe my unexpected presence hindered the robbers. Nevertheless the captain eventually went down and, as he did so, a fist crashed into my face. The last thing I heard before blackness overwhelmed me was a muffled shot.

Thirteen

THE MAKING OF A MILLIONAIRE

I woke to find myself in a bed. My head throbbed, one side being swollen like a melon, and one eye would not open. Feeling the bed beneath me I feared to open the other, for I felt sure that I lay in Hobart Infirmary awaiting shipment to Sydney to be tried for my life. Then the bed moved slightly beneath me and I realised that I lay in a ship riding at anchor.

Slowly I opened my one eye and saw above me the tall skipper of the *Sarah Jane*, his face patched with sticking-plasters. 'Bear up, youngster,' he said. 'You're aboard an American ship and its master is in your debt. You saved my life and the profits of my voyage. If you hadn't hollered and joined in the fight those wharf-rats would have had me down before my boat got to the beach.'

I tried to respond, but my mouth was dry. A plump, pleasant-looking lady appeared and gave me a sip of cordial. 'Don't you press him, Nathan,' she said to the skipper. 'He hardly knows where he is.'

'He knows where he is,' said the captain. 'I've told him, and you can tell me, youngster, how you come to be here. I've seen your back and those tattoos you carry so I know you're a convict boy. After what you did for me I'm not minded to put you back on shore to be beaten or worse. So tell me who you are.'

Thus encouraged I told the captain and his wife my whole story. The recitation brought back to me the grief of my loss and I ended in tears.

'He has had enough,' said the skipper's wife. 'What a dreadful tale!'

'There's no way I could put him ashore now,' said the captain. 'Welcome to the *Sarah Jane*, Jim.'

'Don't forget the penalties, Nathan,' said his wife.

'I surely don't,' he replied, 'but if I stay master of this ship then this boy sails with us.'

I was still fearful of the convict police searching the ship, but Captain Winthrop (for that was his name) seemed so determined to help me escape that I fell asleep happier than I had been since leaving home and only wishing my brave foster-brother had survived to share my good fortune.

A couple of days later, on a Saturday night, the mate dined with us (I had kept to the captain's quarters at his suggestion to avoid visitors to the ship seeing me). We had put away the best of Mrs Winthrop's cooking and the mate and Captain Winthrop fell to business.

'If we can stow the last consignment on Monday morning we'll sail the same day,' said the captain.

'There's no problem there,' said the mate, 'apart from young Jim here.'

The captain stared at him. 'He will be no problem,' he declared.

'Well, I see why you would want to help him after what he did,' said the mate, 'but some of the crew are talking about the fact you've got a convict boy on board and intend to sail with him.'

'And what if I do?' said Captain Winthrop pugnaciously.

'Well, they're talking about the fines – a month's pay off the captain and every man-jack for taking a runaway. That's hard, captain.'

'If Jim isn't found then no one's going to be fined,' the captain declared.

The mate was still uneasy, and my own concern had grown throughout the conversation.

'And what about the reward?' asked the mate. 'Any man can get a month's pay and the right to sign off if he informs on a runaway.'

'If any of my crew is fool enough to drop himself on this Godforsaken island with a month's pay for playing Judas,' said the skipper, 'he'll deal with me before he goes.'

'But we're in Limey waters here,' persisted the mate. 'It's their law.'

'It's their law that sent an innocent boy to the end of the world, cast him in among thieves and murderers and worse and flogged him bloody to make a better Englishman of him,' said the captain. 'You leave the crew and the Limey laws to me, Mister Mate, and you, Jim, I made you a promise and I'll keep it.'

Despite Captain Winthrop's robust response the mate's words had worried me and I passed an uneasy night. On Sunday morning the captain summoned me to join the ship's service. The whole ship's company was paraded on the main-deck in their Sabbath best. Mrs Winthrop read a lesson and played a portative organ while hymns were sung. Many a covert eye was cast on me during the ceremony, for few of the crew had seen me before, and I could not help feeling that some were calculating their chance of earning a month's pay from me.

The hymns done Captain Winthrop stepped forward, his Bible beneath his arm and hands clasped at his back.

'Men,' he said, 'you all know that it's my practice to address a few words to you of a Sunday morning as a kind of sermon. Well, this morning you can stand easy, for I'm going to tell you a story instead.'

Thereupon he launched into the story I had told him of my own misadventure, telling it far better than I could have done so that he drew growls of anger from his audience.

When he had done he called me forward and had me strip off my shirt to show the cane scars across my back.

'Now,' he told the crew, 'I would be failing in my duty as a man and as a Christian if I handed this boy back to the redcoats to hang. So he sails with us tomorrow and any as has anything to say against that can say it now,' and he glowered around him.

The men shuffled their feet, then one spoke up. 'None of us here means any harm to the boy, skipper, but what about the fines if he gets caught aboard? We can't get away without a search—'

'Firstly,' the captain cut him short, 'he ain't a-going to be caught and secondly, if it's the fines that worry you, I'll make you this promise – if the worst came to the worst and he was caught then I should pay all your fines. How does that take you?'

That raised a ragged cheer, but Captain Winthrop was not finished. 'That leaves but one thing,' he said, 'the question of whether any one of you fancies earning a month's pay and his discharge by betraying young Jim to the redcoats. Well, seeing as it's Sunday, let me conclude this service.'

Whipping the Bible from beneath his arm, he opened it and began to read, in tones that rang in the still morning, the verses that tell of the betrayal of Our Lord and the fate of Judas.

'... and his bowels gushed asunder,' he ended, and shut the Book with a snap. 'Now I can't guarantee that such a fate will take any as betrayed young Jim, but I can guarantee that they'll have to deal with me before they gets their discharge and I have little mercy to spare for varmints. And when you've taken your reward and gone ashore you can stay there. You can remain on this damned Limey prison island till you rot, because I shall put the word on you with every master who sails the Pacific.'

He paused and glared around again. 'So, all you know about this boy is that he's my son Jim and by the time the searchers come aboard tomorrow he's going to be mighty sick of something mysterious. Understand?'

'Aye, captain,' a few voices replied and the skipper clapped his braided cap on his head and turned on his heel, leading Mrs Winthrop and me below.

Once in the cabin I asked, 'Will it work, captain?'

He chuckled grimly and his wife laughed outright. 'Bless you,' she said, 'most of the boys on this ship would follow my husband to the Eternal Fire if he told them, and them as wouldn't would rather fetch up in your Port Arthur than look him in the eye when his blood's up.'

'That's very true, Jim,' said the mate, who had followed us below, and my heart began to lift again.

Next morning the last of our cargo was stowed and Captain Winthrop went ashore a final time to report his intention of sailing. In his absence Mrs Winthrop had me back into a bunk, my still-swollen face wrapped in flannel, my eyes rubbed red with my own knuckles and tobacco ash rubbed below my eyes to deepen the sockets.

'Now keep your eyes shut and say nothing,' she instructed me as we heard the captain's boat returning and with it the search boat. Soon there were boots sounding outside the cabin and I knew them to be the soldiers with their convict police and I could not help but be chilled by the thought.

The captain led the two redcoats into the day cabin, next to where I lay, and I heard him tell them, 'Come in for a glass, and tell your gang to keep their smoke away from us. I've a sick boy in the cabin here. He's poorly enough without a dose of British sulphur.'

'A sick boy?' said an English voice. 'What has he got?'

'I wish we knew,' replied the captain. 'He's been too ill to go ashore since we anchored and he gets no better.'

'Did you report him sick when you first landed?' asked the Englishman.

The skipper laughed. 'And me with a cargo to sell? Here, take your glass,' and amid the chink of glasses I thought I heard the different clink of coins.

'We'd best just take a look at him,' said the English voice and I shut my eyes as the cabin door opened. My heart was beating so loudly I would have thought they could hear it through the blankets but I lay still, praying that my eyelids would not flutter.

It seemed an age before the door closed and a voice beyond it said, 'He doesn't look well and that's a fact. Well, we shan't keep you long.'

Nor did they. Soon I heard their boat leaving and a moment later the rattle of the anchor-chain. In a little while the ship was moving, far too slowly for me, out of the harbour.

I stayed in my bunk until Mrs Winthrop came to me, her plump face all aglow with pleasure. 'We're out of the harbour,' she said. 'You can come up on deck now.'

I was quickly on deck and stood at the rail to watch the coast of Van Diemen's Land falling away. I stood, in fact, until long after the land had dropped below the horizon. Then Captain Winthrop came up to my side.

'It's gone, Jim,' he said, 'and we're long out of British waters. You're a free man now.'

I worked my passage across the Pacific, though the skipper did not ask it of me, and I will swear that, as the *Sarah Jane* went from island to island, I grew three inches taller and put on flesh and muscle so that I was no longer even recognisable as the skinny child that had fled from Port Arthur.

At Yerba Bueno in California I took a reluctant farewell of the Winthrops. The captain urged me to stay aboard, but I knew that I dared not venture back into British territory and I could not circumscribe his trading with my fears. So we parted and I have never forgotten their courage and kindliness.

Much of the rest of my tale you already know. I worked as a sailor in American vessels for a while and fought with the Californians against the Spanish. Then, when gold was found in California, I had enough saved to take a quarter share in a claim. It paid enough to finance bigger and yet bigger adventures, until I had more wealth than I could ever spend.

Then I came home to England, intent on using my great wealth to a purpose. That purpose was to prevent, wherever I might, any British child from being dragged into the System and sent abroad. I despaired of politicians, most of whom seemed well-satisfied with the System and ignored any evidence of its inhumanity, vice and corruption, though I financed those few who opposed it. In the main I dispensed my money where I thought it would do the most good for the children of the poor, taking boys and girls from the streets and the poorhouses into education and employment.

When I knelt before Her Majesty and felt her sword touch my shoulder I smiled within myself at the secret thought that she was honouring an orphan convict. At every reverse of the System I have cheered silently. Even the Fenians' escape from Fremantle gladdened me, for no matter what their crimes they had made a joke of the System in the eyes of the world.

I thank the Lord that I have lived to see the System end and even the name of that cursed island vanish. I pray that the black mischief wrought by the System for so many years will soon pass.

As I said in beginning this, I hope that I shall be able to tell you my story myself, but if I am not spared then you must make what you will of this account. Only once have I ever told it all, to your blessed mother before we wed, for I could not marry her in dishonesty. That wonderful lady advised me to tell no other and gave me her hand. I hope that you will be able to receive the truth as gracefully, and I leave to your discretion how much of the contents of this letter you reveal to your sister.

Be that as it may, I enjoin you again to deal with that specified account as I have said, for it belongs to another and those are his wishes. Who he is I am bound not to tell, but he will tell you in good time and when he does he will identify himself to you as "The Man from the Gates of Hell".

Until then you are his trustee. I do not doubt that you will acquit yourself well in that office.

Fourteen

THE RING STRIKES

The little solicitor laid down the last sheet of the manuscript and looked around the table.

'There is no more,' he said, 'apart from an affectionate farewell to Lord Patrick.'

I do not believe that any of us had moved a muscle during the long recitation, apart from Holmes whom I had seen smile to himself now and then, as though at the confirmation of some prediction.

'What an extraordinary narrative!' I exclaimed as I reached for my pipe.

'Quite right, Doctor,' said Lord Patrick, 'and what is just as extraordinary is the extent to which Mr Holmes seems to have divined the content of that document, even to my father's real name.'

Holmes lit his own pipe with slow deliberation. 'Not divined, Lord Backwater, not divined. Were I a reader of tea-leaves or an interpreter of the stars I do not think you would have consulted me.'

'I meant no professional disrespect, I assure you, Mr Holmes,' said the young Lord. 'I was merely expressing my astonishment at the accuracy of your predictions.'

'Oh come now, Holmes,' I said. 'Even I, who have more than a little experience of your methods, cannot see how you knew so much of Lord Backwater's past. Why, before we left Baker Street you were pondering on an Antipodean connection as you called it!'

'And you did not understand the reference,' said Holmes. 'Yet you will recall that I asked Lord Backwater if his father had had any Welsh connections. Both he and Mr Predge said not. That made the Australian interpretation the only reasonable one,' and he applied himself again to his pipe.

The rest of us shared bewildered glances. 'I fear we are all as much in the dark as Mr Watson,' said Lord Backwater.

'When you showed me the note,' said Holmes, 'it referred to the Gates of Hell. There are, I believe two places known by that name. One is a group of rocks in Cardigan Bay, but they are usually named in Welsh. Since it did not seem to be them I inferred that it was the entrance to Port Arthur.'

We all smiled at the simplicity of his explanation and he went on, 'Port Arthur inevitably suggested convicts. When Watson and I came to examine Lord Backwater's body we saw the plainest evidence that Lord Backwater as a young man had been savagely beaten about the back in a way suggestive of the System's punishments. In addition, his forearms revealed those unusual tattoos. Watson will tell you that I have made something of a study of tattoos and Lord Backwater's were instantly recognisable to me as the distinguishing marks of the Ring, whose nature you have heard explained. I confess that I had believed the Ring to be based at Norfolk Island and infered that Lord Backwater had been there as well as at Port Arthur, but we now know that he was spared the ultimate hell of the System.'

'Wonderful!' exclaimed Lord Backwater, while Mr Predge shook his head slowly. 'Mr Holmes, I entirely withdraw any criticisms I have made of your methods. You have been far ahead in this matter from the first. We barely needed my poor father's narrative.'

Holmes acknowledged the apology. 'Oh, but we did,' he said, 'if for no other reason than the fact that it clearly identifies the Man from the Gates of Hell.'

'But he is not named in the document,' I objected.

'Precisely, Watson, and therein lies the identification.'

I was about to protest further when a knock sounded at the door. It was Arnold, Lord Backwater's butler, and his face was grave.

'I beg your pardon for the interruption, My Lord, but I thought you should know that Lady Patricia has not returned from her ride.'

'Not returned?' exclaimed Lord Patrick. 'But it has been hours!' He drew out his watch. 'Good Lord! Where did she go, Arnold?'

'Her Ladyship took her maid Catherine and Tommy the groom with the pony trap, sir,' said Arnold. 'They were going to ride around the lakes for the afternoon, but it is well up to dinner-time and there is no sign of them.'

'Then she has evidently met with some accident or delay,' said Lord Backwater. 'Arnold, we must search the park at once while there is light. Call the ground staff and the grooms. I shall go with them. Mr Holmes, Doctor, I am sorry to involve you in a domestic matter but I would value your assistance.'

'Gladly,' said Holmes, 'and I hope you are right that this is only a domestic matter.'

'What do you mean, Mr Holmes?' demanded Lord Patrick.

'Only that this mishap to Lady Patricia follows too closely upon other events. I have told you, Lord Backwater, coincidences are rarely what they seem.'

On foot and on horseback, until it grew dark and after dark by lantern-light, the sprawling grounds of Backwater Hall were searched minutely that evening, but no trace could be found of the missing trio or their vehicle.

It was nearly midnight before Lord Backwater called off the search. We were making our way wearily through the yard of the Hall when a groom dashed up to us.

'Lord Backwater!' he called. 'The trap's been found.'

'Where?' demanded Lord Patrick.

'It was tied up to a tree by the North Pool,' said the groom. 'There was no damage nor nothing but there wasn't any trace of Her Ladyship neither.'

'But we went out past the North Pool while it was still light. It was not there then. What can this mean, Mr Holmes?' asked Lord Backwater.

'I fear that it confirms my foreboding,' said Holmes. 'The conveyance has been left as a message. Still, there is nothing that can be done now, except perhaps to send word to Inspector Scott to attend you in the morning now that we are sure we are dealing with another crime.'

'My poor sister!' exclaimed the young nobleman. 'Are these the same fiends that slew my father? What will they do with Patricia?'

Holmes touched Lord Patrick's arm. 'Do not disturb yourself unnecessarily, My Lord. Lady Patricia will come to no harm. Our villains require something of you and will have taken her as a hostage. There is no purpose in doing her harm. You must possess yourself in patience until we can learn more of their intentions.'

Even after that exhausting and eventful day I doubt if any of us at Backwater Hall slept easily that night. Certainly I found my slumbers delayed by reflections on the day's occurrences and when I did sleep it was restlessly.

When we gathered in the breakfast room next morning I saw that Inspector Scott had been summoned on Holmes' advice. Once we had taken our food from the sideboard and sat down, Lord Backwater addressed the table.

'There has been a letter,' he said. 'It arrived during the night.'

'May I see it?' asked Holmes, and Lord Patrick passed it across.

Holmes held it up to the morning sunlight. 'A single sheet of cheap quarto, written in decent roundhand with a fair pen,' he said. 'It tells us very little.'

'And the message?' I asked.

He read it aloud. '"Lord Backwater, the Black Queen belonged to us by right and by oath and we shall have our compensation. Be assured that your sister is safe and will remain so if we have what is ours, no more. You shall hear from us again."'

He handed the paper back to Lord Backwater. 'At the bottom are the unmistakable mottoes of the Ring – "On the square Ever" and "On the cross Never".'

'What on earth is the Black Queen?' I asked.

'There I am as much in the dark as you, Watson. We know that it is the name of the account at Barings which the late Lord Backwater left in trust to Lord Patrick on someone else's behalf. I had speculated that it might be the name of a mine somewhere, but that is pure guesswork.'

'What will you do now, Mr Holmes?' asked Inspector Scott.

'I fear that yesterday's events make it imperative that I leave as soon as possible. Perhaps Lord Backwater will be good enough to arrange for me to catch the mid-morning train.'

His reply fell like a thunderbolt on the table. 'Leave as soon as possible?' exclaimed Lord Backwater and I with one voice.

'You cannot leave us now,' said Lord Patrick. 'Now that we know that my sister is in the hands of this villainous secret society. I am relying upon you to guide me, Mr Holmes.'

'I apologise for surprising you, Lord Backwater,' said my friend, 'but

I reached certain conclusions during the night and the confirmation that your sister is a prisoner of the Ring merely makes my actions more urgent. I must be in London as rapidly as possible.'

An appalled silence reigned around the breakfast table as each of us struggled to absorb this new turn of events. Holmes downed his coffee and rose from the table.

'I shall leave Watson here to assist you,' he said. 'As to forthcoming events, it is easy to deduce that you will soon hear from the Ring again, specifying what it is that they want of you and offering terms of exchange for your sister. It is not for me to command you, Lord Backwater, but I urge you most solemnly to enter into no exchange for Lady Patricia until I return.'

'But when will that be?' I asked.

'What I have in mind should only take a day or two,' he replied. 'I am sure you will hold the fort for me that little time,' and he smiled and walked out of the room.

The little group at the table broke up and we followed Lord Backwater disconsolately into the library. There we discussed every aspect of the case but without gaining any further insight into events. Inspector Scott remained at the Hall as the day wore on, lest another message should arrive, but none had come by evening. I was taking a farewell of him in the hall when Arnold approached.

'Excuse me, Doctor,' he said, 'but while you were out searching last night there was a message for Mr Holmes, and I'm afraid that with all the worry over Her Ladyship it went clear out of my mind.'

'Perhaps you had better let me have the message,' I said.

'It was Williams, sir – the strange old man who plays the fiddle at the Backwater Arms. He came up to the Hall during the search and said he wanted a word with Mr Holmes. When he was told Mr Holmes was out with the search parties he left no word but just took himself off.'

I thanked Arnold and lost no time in conveying this information to Lord Backwater.

'Perhaps the old scoundrel's conscience has finally struck him,' said Inspector Scott, 'and he wants to assist us.'

'Maybe he is merely the Ring's messenger,' I hazarded. 'After all, he guided the murderers to the beech glade and I have seen the Ring's marks upon him with my own eyes.'

'What will you do?' asked Lord Patrick.

'I shall go and see Williams,' I said, 'and see what he wishes to say.'

'I should not go to tonight, if I were you,' said the Inspector. 'This may be merely an excuse for an ambush. If you will wait till morning I shall join you and we can go together.'

We agreed on this manoeuvre and Inspector Scott left to report to Colonel Caddage, while Lord Backwater and I passed the evening with a game of billiards that both of us were too distracted to play well.

Fifteen

THE SCARLET "J"

Even the brightness of a summer morning could not pierce the gloom of the track to Tin-Fiddle Williams' shack, and my previous experience along that way led me to step cautiously, probing any clump of leaves with my stick and keeping one hand on the pistol in my coat pocket. Inspector Scott walked behind me with his policeman's eyes alert for any sign of an ambush but we reached the clearing by the pool with no trouble.

No smoke was drifting from the makeshift chimney of the hut as we made towards it.

'That's queer!' said the Inspector suddenly. 'The door's not shut. That's not like old Williams.'

I could see that the door of the shack had been left slightly ajar.

'We should go a bit careful, Doctor,' said Scott.

I drew my pistol and, as softly as we could walk on the carpet of dried leaves, we crept up on the door.

Standing either side of the entrance we could not see any distance through the slight opening and no sound reached our ears from within.

'I don't like this a bit,' whispered the Inspector, and knocked on the door with his fist, at the same calling out, 'Williams! It's Inspector Scott and Dr Watson.' There was still no sound from inside. Scott nodded to me after a moment and I pushed the door further open with my pistol. It swung unresisted and I stepped cautiously inside.

If Williams' hut had been a shambles when last I saw it, it was more so now. All the myriad contents of that magpie's lair seemed to have been tumbled and overturned in all directions. Miraculously an unharmed lamp was still burning on a rickety shelf. There was only one space left in the hut and that was filled by the body of Tin-Fiddle Williams.

The old convict lay face down on the earthen floor and it took no medical expertise to see that he was dead, felled by a series of savage blows that had left his head a bloody mess. His outstretched left hand grasped the neck of his precious and unique instrument and, in the shock of the discovery, I noted the apparent irrelevance that he held it in the wrong hand.

Inspector Scott was searching carefully through the debris about us. 'He put up a tremendous battle,' he observed. 'The place was wrecked while they fought. Was he attacked by one man or more?'

'So far as I can tell,' I said, 'he has been struck across both sides of the head, which suggests two attackers, though not necessarily.'

He continued to poke about among the wreckage and suddenly made an exclamation of pleasure.

'Look here!' he said and pointed to broken glass in a corner. 'You can see how that ramshackle table has collapsed and taken everything on it to the ground. That glass was a rum bottle from its shape and colour, and there – see – three tin cups scattered.' He borrowed my stick to hook the cups out of the littered corner.

'Sure enough,' he said when he had examined them. 'There were three of them – Williams and two guests. They drank rum and then, perhaps when they thought they'd got him drunk enough, they beat him down. When do you think he died, Doctor?'

I had been completing my examination of the body. 'I doubt if he lived long with injuries such as these,' I said, 'but when they were inflicted is another question. I can only guess, but the body is cold and the death rigor has passed off, so I imagine that he died last night.'

The Inspector nodded. 'The lamp would suggest that as well,' he agreed. 'So they feared he was going to tell on them and silenced the poor old wretch.'

He gazed around him. 'I don't think we shall learn much more here,' he said, then paused as his eye fell on Williams' hand clutching the fiddle. 'What do you think those marks mean, Doctor?'

I looked again at the instrument. I had noted before that its metal back, which lay uppermost, was bloodstained, but so was much that was in the vicinity of the corpse.

'I don't know. Perhaps he had it in his hand when they struck him or maybe he grabbed at it as a weapon to defend himself.'

'I think not, Doctor. They wouldn't have struck him while he was holding something and the last thing on earth he would have used as a weapon was his precious fiddle. Besides, those marks aren't splashes. Look!'

Now I realised that there were five distinct marks on the polished metal surface and they appeared to have been made with Williams' own bloodstained hand. The largest mark appeared to be the letter "J" scrawled in script and to its right lay four further blobs of blood. I could not make head or tail of it, but I took out my pocket-book and began to draw the pattern carefully for I knew that Holmes would require an account of it and who knew what meaning he might extract from it. My diagram is herewith:

'So he lived long enough to try and leave us a message,' mused the Inspector. 'A "J" and what then? Are those blobs meant to be letters? Was he so far gone he could make no other letters? Did he mean "J" and four letters following? It is too much for me. I shall have it photographed and let Mr Holmes enlighten us when he returns.'

Shortly afterwards we left the hut and separated at the road, Inspector Scott to arrange for a photograph of the violin and the removal of Williams' body, I to return to Backwater Hall.

I reported to Lord Backwater the results of the morning's excursion and he heard me out, but without offering opinion or comment and with, I believed, a slight air of impatience.

'So we do not know what he would have told us,' he said when I had finished my account. 'No matter, perhaps, for we have heard further from the Ring.'

'Indeed?' I said. 'Have they set out any terms?'

'Oh yes,' said Lord Patrick. 'If you do not mind waiting for Predge to arrive I think we should confer as to our response.'

Predge arrived in time to take luncheon with us and afterwards we repaired to the library. Lord Backwater read us the latest message from the Ring, delivered by an unseen messenger in mid-morning.

'"Lord Backwater, we have told you that, through no fault of your own, you are in possession of what belongs to us. The proceeds of the Black Queen do not belong to you. We believe that our interest in what you hold amounts to some twenty-five thousand pounds sterling, but we have been put to extraordinary lengths to collect our dues and, in consequence, require the addition of a further twenty-five thousand pounds"'

'Damnably cool!' I interjected.

'They hold the whip hand at present. They can afford insolence. Let me continue,' and he read on: '"If you are sensible and wish to safeguard your sister, you will adopt the following plan. On the day that this is delivered you will have the money, in Treasury notes, placed in a canvas sack. Let us have no nonsense with marked notes. We are all men of honour. The sack should be firmly attached to a long rope. Take them to the bridge over the South Pool and lay the sack exactly in the centre of the bridge. Pass the rope from the sack along the bridge to the south, leaving its end by the great oak that stands close to the bridge. It would be as well if the rope is at least the length of the bridge. At dusk you may be on the north end of the bridge. If there is anyone on the south side of the pool or on the bridge there will be no transaction. Precisely at sunset your sister and her maid will be tied to the free end of the rope and permitted to walk across the bridge as the sack is drawn to the southern end. If all goes well you shall have her back unharmed. If you attempt to betray the operation she will be shot down. If there is any attempt at pursuit after the exchange, your groom will die. These arrangements are quite straightforward. If we see the sack and rope on the bridge at sunset we shall know that you have accepted them. If not, we shall be pleased to draw our own conclusions and act accordingly."'

'And it ends with the cross and square rigmarole,' said Lord Patrick, dropping the letter to the table.

'This is preposterous,' I said. 'You will not, I take it, fall in with their demands?'

'I really see no other choice,' said Lord Backwater.

'But surely even you cannot raise such a sum in hours?' I asked, hoping to delay on the grounds of practical difficulties.

'But I can,' he replied. 'As soon as I received the letter I sent for Predge. He confirms that the amount is inconsiderable in terms of the estate. My bank has been wired to prepare the notes and Arnold has been sent with my note to collect it.'

'But what if this is an attempt at theft?' I asked. 'Arnold may be waylaid and robbed.'

'He is accompanied by three armed grooms and I have little doubt that he will soon return with the money, Doctor. It only remains to make our dispositions for this evening.'

Aware of Holmes' solemn warning I was at a loss for a way of carrying out his advice. 'You will recall that Sherlock Holmes warned you against any exchange in his absence,' I said.

'I have nothing but respect for Mr Holmes' intelligence, Doctor, but he is not here when he might have been. I, on the other hand, have to rescue my sister from her captors by any means at my disposal. If that is as easy as the spending of money, then I must do it. My father would expect no less of me.'

'Your father would not have expected you to fall into a trap set by the Ring,' I said.

'If you can see the trap, then by all means point it out to me, Doctor. Unless you can do so, I shall carry on.'

'Why have they selected the bridge?' I asked.

'The pool there is fed by a stream from the east that drains it on the west. At both ends the stream is wide and deep. Without using the bridge it is impossible to cross the water without a detour of about a mile in either direction.'

'Then they cannot be pursued. They seem to know the ground well,' I remarked. 'I do not like the idea that they are choosing the field of play.'

'It is no use, Doctor,' said Mr Predge. 'I have urged His Lordship to consider Mr Holmes' advice or, at the very least, to involve the police, but he will not hear of it.'

'Patricia is my sister, gentlemen,' said Lord Patrick. 'You must allow me to act as I think best. Nevertheless, Doctor, and in spite of your objections, I would value your assistance if you will give it.'

With a sense of foreboding I agreed.

Sixteen

THE BRIDGE AT TWILIGHT

The South Pool of Backwater Park in daylight is a place of great charm, fringed with bullrushes and spread with water-lilies. On its north side a carriageway runs along most of the shore, crossing the pool by a narrow ornamental bridge some one hundred yards long towards the eastern end. While the northern carriageway runs through open grassland at the shore, once it has crossed the bridge it plunges into an ancient part of the thick woods that clothe much of the park to the south.

Shortly before sunset I accompanied Lord Backwater to the northern end of the bridge. With us came three armed grooms. There was no sign of activity when we arrived.

The money sack had been prepared and now we attached it to a length of rope and carefully set it in the middle of the bridge. Following the instructions in the letter, we carried the end of the rope to the southern limit of the bridge and laid it beside the specified area. With a last glance around us we retreated to the north side.

Anxiously we watched the sun slipping down behind the trees at the western end of the lake, the silence broken only by the occasional croaking of frogs and the rippling of the breeze in the reeds about the shore. Light dwindled from the sky and soon it became impossible for our eyes to pierce the dark tunnel opposite us where the carriageway disappeared into the woods. At last the sun vanished entirely, so that the scene was lit only by the reflection of the sky from the pool.

Lord Backwater and I were pacing nervously about the bridge's northern abutment and I had just lit a cigarette when a voice hailed us from the far side.

'Lord Backwater!' it cried. 'If you are ready to make the exchange, raise your right arm.'

Both of us strained our eyes but could see nobody across the bridge. Lord Patrick raised his arm and called, 'Let me see my sister and her servants!'

Now we saw movement under the trees and a small group of figures emerged into the light. Two heavily built men in rough clothing and soft hats flanked the group, and between them stood two young women and a youth, their hands apparently tied behind their backs and handkerchiefs bound across their mouths.

'They have come to no harm,' the same voice called, 'and there will be none so long as you stick to our terms. We shall tie the young ladies to the end of the rope.'

'Watch the money-bag,' Lord Patrick commanded the grooms. 'If there is to be false play this is where it will occur.

'Proceed very slowly!' he called across the bridge. 'You must know there are guns on you.'

'There will be no tricks,' came the reply. 'Wait now while we make our arrangements.'

We watched while the two girls were attached to the rope, about two paces apart. They were led round the back of the tree while one of the men held the rope.

'Lord Backwater,' our communicant called, 'I am going to pay out the rope around the tree and allow the young ladies to walk across to you. So long as the bag comes back to us there should be no difficulty.'

Lady Patricia and her maid began to advance slowly across the bridge as the man by the tree let out the rope. When the slack of the rope was taken up, the canvas sack of money began to inch towards the far shore. Suddenly there was a disturbance. The bound and gagged youth, whom I took to be Tommy the groom, seemed to be struggling to escape. My heart went out to the poor lad, realising his fellow prisoners were about to be freed and not knowing his own fate.

Lord Backwater stepped forward. 'Tommy!' His voice rang sharply across the water. 'Bear up, lad. You are my sister's safeguard in this and I shall not forget you. I promise you that I shall not rest until you are safe.'

The boy abandoned his struggles and the exchange went on. The rate at which the rope was paid around the tree governed the speed of the operation and the man at the rope seemed to be in no hurry. Foot by foot the canvas bag slid away from us and pace by pace the girls stepped towards us.

'Your Lordship,' muttered one of the grooms, 'when that bag reaches the far end and Her Ladyship is at this end, couldn't we rush them? There's five of us here.'

'Tommy would die instantly,' said Lord Patrick, 'and we should be shot down before we were half-way across the bridge. We are in the open here and they can see better than we can, even in this light.'

'Besides,' I added, 'we cannot tell how many more of them there may be in the darkness under those trees.'

Nevertheless I sympathised with the groom's impatience. It was completely galling to stand impotently while the scoundrels across the pool drew the ransom nearer and nearer to their hands.

The slow movement of the young ladies across the pool had taken so long that the light was now almost gone and my unease deepened with the darkness. All seemed to be proceeding smoothly, but Holmes' warning still echoed in my mind.

At last the girls were almost within our grasp, but still Lord Backwater held the grooms back, ordering them to light lanterns.

A jerk on the far end of the rope brought the girls up short, only two paces from us. Out of the inky darkness across the pool the voice called again.

'We are cutting the bag free. When I call again you can take the ladies. If all has been done properly we shall release the boy in the morning.'

'If you harm that boy I shall personally seek you out and kill you!' replied Lord Backwater, and I knew that he meant it.

A laugh floated across to us. 'Never fear,' said the voice. 'The bag is ours and the ladies are yours. Good night, Your Lordship.'

The grooms lifted their lanterns and Lord Patrick and I sprang forward to receive Lady Patricia and her maid.

With my pocket-knife I slit the gag around the maid's jaw. Tears were streaming down her face and, as I freed her hands, she was struggling to find words.

Behind me I heard a sharp oath from Lord Patrick. Swinging around I saw the cause of his alarm. He too had freed the other prisoner and the lanterns' light revealed that he now held the groom Tommy dressed in Lady Patricia's clothes.

'Oh, Your Lordship!' cried Catherine. 'Lady Patricia is still there. They made her dress as Tommy and they've still got her!' and she burst into loud sobs.

The groom and I had to restrain Lord Backwater from plunging across the bridge into the blackness that now enveloped the far woods.

It was a silent and gloomy party that made its way back to Backwater Hall and, once there, I busied myself with ensuring that Tommy and Catherine had not suffered by their experience. Both were, at least, able to assure Lord Backwater that his sister had been unharmed when they left her beside the bridge.

His Lordship's mood swung like a pendulum. At one moment he paced the floor, raging incoherently against his sister's abductors, at another he would slump into a chair and stare in morose silence at the floor.

When I had attended to the boy and girl and sent them to their beds I poured Lord Patrick a large brandy. 'This will not do,' I told him as I pressed the glass into his nerveless hand. 'There is nothing to be done tonight, Lord Patrick, and you are overwrought. We must get a good night's rest and prepare a new plan in the morning.'

He swallowed the brandy and looked up at me with dulled eyes.

'You are quite right of course, Doctor. We shall meet again at breakfast. Good night, Doctor.'

I watched him walk away across the room, his shoulders bowed and the youth entirely gone from his step. He turned back at the door.

'I apologise, Doctor. I have not thanked you for standing by me at the bridge, despite your misgivings.'

You may imagine that our meeting at breakfast was scarcely more cheerful. Both of us picked at our food and barely spoke, each not knowing how to raise the topic of the previous night's failure.

A rattle of gravel outside the windows alerted us to the arrival of a vehicle. It was a dogcart from the station and, a moment later, Arnold was at the door.

'Mr Sherlock Holmes, sir,' he announced and he had barely spoken the words when my friend strode into the room.

'Good morning, Lord Backwater, Watson,' he greeted us. 'Is there any coffee to spare? The refreshment room at Swindon in the early morning is not the best place to break one's fast.'

Without waiting for an answer he made for the side-board and commenced loading a plate. I was surprised, for I had long observed that Holmes' appetite seemed to vanish when a case was going badly and only returned when he was making progress, but I reflected that he could not yet be aware of last night's fiasco. Nevertheless I was deeply relieved to see him.

He joined us at the table and Arnold poured his coffee. As my friend ate, Lord Backwater outlined the events of the previous day. I watched Holmes' face during the recital but it betrayed nothing. When the story was done, he wiped his mouth and laid down his napkin, gazing at me across the table.

'Well, Watson,' he said, 'you seem to have made a pretty botch of this affair!'

Lord Backwater sprang to my defence.

'You must not blame the Doctor, Mr Holmes. He was urgent in his entreaties that I stand by your advice, but I could only think of my poor sister in the hands of the Ring.'

'That is precisely why I warned you,' said Holmes. 'I was fully aware that your emotional involvement would make you a prey to dangerous impulses and that a cool head was needed to assess the situation.'

'Really, Holmes,' I protested, 'I do not see what more I might have done. Once Lord Backwater had made his decision every precaution was taken and I do not see how we could have detected a trap.'

'No, Watson, you do not see because you have not trained your mind to understand what you see. Did it not strike you as strange that the exchange was fixed for sunset? There is no time of day when the light is more misleading. The method of exchange could have been employed at any time, but they chose sunset because they wished to hide something. Even then the situation might have been saved. Did the gags not warn you?'

'I do not understand how they should have warned us,' I replied.

'They should have shown you that the villains did not wish you to hear the prisoners' voices or something that they might say, that they wanted you to rely on dimly seen shapes in gathering darkness.'

'I do not know what else might have been done,' I grumbled.

'As soon as the message was received there might have been armed men posted in the woods around the bridge, so that anyone approaching it could be surrounded. The bag could have been booby-trapped so that it would distract them when they examined it.'

'Then, if you would have had so many ideas, it is the more pity that you took yourself off,' I remarked, a trifle huffily, I admit.

'I took myself off, as you put it, Watson, because there were matters which I had to attend to in London. Those things are done and will, I trust, bear interesting fruit in the near future,' replied Holmes.

In the virtual certainty of further criticism I drew Holmes' attention to the death of the old fiddler. He listened to my account of how Scott and I had found the old man, then examined the sketch I had made of the blood-marked violin.

'Scott and I wondered if he had written the "J", then attempted four other letters and failed,' I said.

'I doubt it,' said Holmes. 'The "J", although a degree misshapen, is strongly scrawled. The blobs are each clear and distinct. They show no sign of trailing away. Each has been made with a single firm touch of the finger. It seems the old fiddler summoned his last resource to leave this sign.'

He examined the paper a while longer, then folded it into his own pocket-book.

'We shall see Inspector Scott's photograph in due course,' he said, 'and, in the meantime, we cannot spare too much time to speculate on what Williams might have told us had chance allowed. We must turn our attention to rescuing Lady Patricia.'

'What do you think they will do next?' asked Lord Backwater.

'They will offer another exchange, for a further sum of money, in due course. When they do so, Lady Patricia will be in great danger.'

'Why more so than now?' I queried.

'Because they cannot perform last night's trick twice. A second exchange will be offered solely in an attempt to acquire a further sum of money. Whether they achieve that purpose or not they will have to consider disposing of the lady. If they were to succeed in a second ruse they would know that they could not achieve a third success and she would become unnecessary to them. Even more so if a second attempt fails.'

He looked at our glum faces.

'Come, gentlemen,' he said, 'last night has not been an entire loss. You may have bought them at a pretty price, Lord Backwater, but we now have two witnesses. Perhaps when I have had another cup of coffee we might see what Tommy and Catherine can tell us.'

Seventeen

HUNTING THE LADY

Both Tom and Catherine seemed to have suffered no lasting ill effects from their capture when Arnold brought them to the library, though they were understandably nervous when introduced to their employer's consulting detective.

Holmes smiled at them as they sat, each erect on a hard-backed chair.

'I hope,' he said, 'that a night's rest has helped you to recover from your adventures.'

'Oh yes, sir,' they both answered simultaneously.

'Now, Tom,' Holmes continued, 'you were driving Lady Patricia and Catherine. Perhaps you should start the story. Tell us what happened.'

'Well, sir, us had been to Lord Backwater's funeral, sir, and Mr Patrick – that is Lord Patrick, sir – he said we could take the afternoon off after church. So I went back to the stables with the horses and while I was there Catherine came along and said Lady Patricia fancied a bit of fresh air and she knew it was an afternoon off but there was a shilling in it if I'd take 'em round the park. So I took the pony trap round to the front with Catherine and Lady Patricia come and got in. I asked her if

110

she fancied anywhere particular, but Lady Patricia just said to drive about wherever I thought. So I went out to the North Pool and round beyond it, intending to come down the far side of South Pool and back through the 'zalea plantation.'

'Just wait one minute, Tom,' said Holmes. 'Lord Backwater, have you a map of the park to hand?'

Lord Patrick rose and went to a shelf, returning with a marbled slip-case from which he drew a folded map. 'I think', he said, 'that this is of sufficient scale to help you follow Tom's descriptions,' and he spread out the map where Holmes and I could both see it.

'Thank you,' said Holmes. 'Please go on, young man.'

'Well, we was in that piece they call the Lawyer's Walk, between the South Woods and the 'zaleas, where the carriageway bends a bit sharp and you can't see beyond the bend 'cause of the leaves. I always go a bit slow along there and I'd just taken the bend slowly when a chap steps out of the bushes, calm as you like, and takes Blossom's head. Now I thought something was wrong right away for I never saw the chap before and I didn't like the way he just took hold of my horse. If he wanted me to stop I wasn't going fast, he could've asked.'

'What did you do?' asked Holmes.

'Oh, Tommy was ever so brave, Mr Holmes,' broke in Catherine. 'He stood up and he took up his whip and he said, "What are you doing with my horse? Who are you? I'll have you know this is Lord Backwater's sister I'm driving."'

'He laughed,' said Tommy. 'He laughed at me and said, "Put down that whip and jump down!" and he pulled a great pistol from his pocket and pointed it at me. I was still going to go at him with the whip, but Lady Patricia says, "Do as he says, Tommy. I don't wish to see you hurt." So I put the whip up and jumped down.'

'What manner of man was he?' asked Holmes. 'How was he

dressed? How did he speak?'

'He was a big, broad-shouldered fellow with a scruff of beard and moustache. He had corduroys and a felt hat.'

'He spoke funny,' interjected Catherine. 'He wasn't from round here. He sounded like a North Countryman.'

'That sounds like the man who controlled last night's ceremony,' I observed. 'I thought the voice had a tinge of Lancashire about it.'

'There cannot be all that many Brothers of the Ring in England,' said Holmes. 'Its capital was Norfolk Island and few have ever returned from there. They must, I imagine, call in their Brothers from all over England when necessary. What happened next?' he asked of Tommy.

'When he'd got me down from the trap and had his gun on me another chap appeared out of the bushes. He was much the same as the first in appearance, only a bit smaller. He had a pistol already in his hand. He put a blindfold on me and bound my hands behind me. Then I heard them doing the same to Cathy and Her Ladyship.'

He paused, I could see the anger that still worked in the boy at the capture of his charges.

'When we was all blinded,' he continued, 'they put us all in the trap and one of them drove. Now you're going to want to know where we went, sir, but that's difficult.'

'Because of the blindfolds?' I said.

'Not entirely, sir,' he said. 'I growed up in Backwater Woods and I'd say I knows them as well as any, even with my eyes shut. But they bewildered me at the outset. They turned the trap back along the way we'd come at first, but there's a six-ways cross between the Lawyer's Walk and South Woods and when we got there they drove round and round it before they turned off, so I couldn't think which way we'd turned.'

Holmes had his long forefinger on the map, resting at the junction to which the boy had referred.

112

'I think we went along the ride that goes down the side of South Woods and came round the back,' said Catherine.

Tommy so far forgot himself in the presence of his employer as to demand, 'How do you know, then?'

'I been thinking,' she said, 'and it was the smell. There's no pines in the South Woods, but there are along the outside of that ride and I could smell them all the time.'

Holmes followed her suggestion with his finger on the plan. 'And where do you think you went next?' he enquired.

Tommy shook his head and the maid looked crestfallen. 'I don't rightly know, sir. We lost the smell of the pines, so I suppose we come to the end of that ride by Anne's Cross, but then we turned on to grass.'

'Which way did you turn?' Holmes interrupted.

'Left,' said Tommy promptly.

'So,' said my friend, thoughtfully, 'you left the woods and turned back towards the heart of the estate. Tell me,' he continued, after a pause to study the map, 'did you cross either of the canal bridges?'

'No, sir,' said Tommy. 'We was driving over grass till we got there.'

'And where was "there"?' asked Holmes.

'Where they was taking us,' said the boy. 'We was on the grass for a long time before we stopped. Then they had us down and led us down some steps.'

'Steps!' exclaimed Holmes. 'Wooden ones? Brick ones?'

'Brick ones, I think,' said Tommy. 'They took us down them steps and into a big, hollow place where their voices echoed. It was cold in there and it smelled old and musty-like.'

Holmes was poring over the map. He looked up at Lord Backwater. 'If Catherine is correct, they were somewhere in the open grassland to the north-west of the woods,' he said, 'and if they were in a cellar, then there must surely be a building, or the remains of a building. I see only Park Farm in that vicinity. Could that be it?'

Lord Patrick shook his head. 'Park Farm is tenanted,' he said, 'and there are no other buildings in that area.'

'What about the cellars of the Old Hall?' I suggested.

'The Old Hall was, indeed, in that area, but my father had the cellars filled in and the last traces above ground removed. There is a small stand of elms now where Backwater Old Hall stood.'

'Were you kept underground all the time?' asked Holmes of the two youngsters.

'Yes, sir,' said Tommy. 'There seemed to be two big rooms in there and Lady Patricia and Cathy was put in the far one and I was kept near the bottom of the steps, but we never saw the place for we was kept blindfolded all the time.'

'How did they feed you?' I asked.

'Only bread and cheese and water,' said Catherine, 'and they wouldn't even take the blindfolds off for us to eat.'

Holmes looked up from the map. 'Is there anything else you recall? How were you taken to the bridge last night?'

'I think it was the same way as we went, sir,' said Tommy. 'If Cathy's right, sir, it was across the grass and round the back drive, then through the South Wood to the pool.'

'And you don't believe you ever left the park?' asked Holmes.

'If they did not cross the canal bridges they cannot have done,' said Lord Backwater. 'The only other way out would be past the North Lodge and the gate there is manned.'

'Thank you both,' said Holmes to the youngsters. 'Tommy, you have nothing to reproach yourself with. I'm sure Lord Backwater agrees that you did your very best to protect your charges. Catherine, your information has been a great help to us,' and, as the boy and girl stood up to leave, he slipped a coin into the hand of each.

The door had barely closed behind them when there was a timid tap upon it and Catherine returned.

'I beg your pardon, My Lord, Mr Holmes, but there is one thing more.'

'Yes?' said Holmes. 'Tell us anything you think.'

'Tommy wouldn't have known it because he was in the first room by the steps, but our room was different.'

'In what way?' asked Holmes.

'There was a draught, a cold draught, sometimes from one end, and sometimes I thought we were near water.'

'By one of the pools?' I said.

'I'm sure I don't know. I just thought of water when that draught blew. That's all I can recall.'

Holmes smiled. 'You are a very bright young lady,' he said, 'and with your help we shall rescue your mistress,' and he showed her from the room again.

'You sound very sure of yourself,' said Lord Backwater when the door had closed again.

'If your sister has not left the park,' said Holmes, 'then it should not be impossible to find her before the Ring moves again.'

'Do you make anything of their evidence?' I asked.

'The boy is a practical country lad and told us what he is sure of, the girl added her feminine impressions. I have said before, Watson, that I would give all of my trained ratiocinative processes for the intuition of even a simple country lass like Catherine. Women have senses that they do not even know.'

He looked at the map again. 'You are sure,' he said to Lord Backwater, 'that there are no derelict buildings, no follies, no ruins, no burial chambers or such anywhere in the park?'

Lord Backwater shook his head emphatically. 'Nothing that remotely accords with their description. Are they right, do you think?'

'Their testimony is confusing in the light of the plan and your information, but I suspect they will reveal the answer. Now, I shall be grateful if you and Watson will leave me to ponder on this plan.'

He lit his pipe as we left, and settled back to the map. Lord Backwater and I took ourselves to the billiard room until the luncheon gong. Holmes did not join us in the dining-room and during the afternoon, I looked into the library to see him shrouded in tobacco smoke and surrounded by scribbled sketches.

'Will he remain like that long?' enquired Lord Backwater.

'I have known Sherlock Holmes sit motionless and smoke pipe after pipe for a day and two nights when wrestling with a particularly thorny problem,' I said, 'but he will unravel it in the end.'

When the dinner gong sounded I managed to bully Holmes into dressing and appearing at table, though his appetite was non-existent. I did not question him for his attitude made it clear that he had not yet solved the problem.

The dessert was a delicious confection of summer fruits and ice. Holmes refused it, but I took one mouthful and remarked on it to our host.

'The fruits are from the Hall's gardens and, of course, my father had refrigeration equipment installed, so we do not have to rely on Cook's willingness to wind one of those tedious ice-makers,' he replied.

Holmes, who had played only a minimal part in our conversation at table, suddenly looked up. 'Refrigeration!' he exclaimed and snapped his fingers. 'Refrigeration, of course!'

Lord Patrick and I stared at him in amazement, but he ignored us and turned to Arnold who stood by the buffet. 'Arnold,' he said, 'I have done less than justice to Cook's work. Perhaps I should have a large portion of her dessert, after all.'

When it was served he set to with a will, while Lord Backwater and I exchanged bewildered glances. I knew only that the sudden return of his appetite signalled a successful end to his ponderings.

At last he put aside his plate. 'Now,' he said, 'I believe I can tell you where Lady Patricia is being held. The answer was in that delicious dessert which I so unthinkingly spurned. Arnold, would you be so good as to fetch my papers and the plan from the library?'

Eighteen

INTO BATTLE

When my friend had scattered his papers over much of the dining-table he said, 'I had forgotten that Inspector Scott told us that your father installed the latest refrigeration mechanisms, Lord Backwater, so that you do not require an ice-house.'

'That is true,' said Lord Patrick, 'but I confess I cannot see how that will help us.'

'But Backwater Old Hall had no such modern arrangements,' continued Holmes.

Suddenly I saw where his thoughts were bending. 'An ice-house!' I exclaimed.

'Well done, Watson! That is undoubtedly the answer. Somewhere in the park lies the former ice-house of the Old Hall,' said Holmes.

'I'm sure you are right,' said Lord Patrick, frowning, 'but I have no idea where it might be. My father's mechanisms were installed when this house was built and we never had any occasion to be aware of any ice-house.'

'Then we must find someone who recalls the park as it was in Squire

Varley's days,' said Holmes.

Arnold, who had been attempting to serve the coffee amidst the litter that Holmes had made of the dining-table, coughed discreetly.

'Perhaps I may be of assistance, Mr Holmes. My first position was as a pantry-boy with Squire Varley.'

Holmes turned to him, his eyes bright. 'There was an ice-house?' he demanded.

'Oh yes, sir. A large one. Before Mr Rupert's loss the Squire was a great entertainer. We had a big ice-house.'

'And where was it?' asked Holmes.

'If I might just see the plan, sir,' said Arnold, and delicately removing the sugar bowl which Holmes had used as a paperweight he looked it over for a moment.

'I would say it was in that vicinity,' he said at last, pointing to a spot on the map. 'It lay by the canal because that is how the ice was brought in, sir.'

'But its entrance must have long vanished,' protested Lord Backwater. 'I know every inch of the park and I've never come across it.'

'I think, sir, that it can still be located. The canal, if Your Lordship recalls, enters the park by the West Tunnel under a long rise in the land. The ice-house lay below that rise and close to its entrance was one of the large cedars that Squire Varley's father had planted.'

'So you could take us to it?' asked Lord Backwater.

'I should be pleased to, sir,' said Arnold.

'What sort of a place was it?' asked Holmes.

'There were steps down to the entrance in the slope, sir, with a door at the bottom. Inside there were two chambers, both walled in brick, and connected by an archway, and at the back was a short passage that led to the landing-place in the West Tunnel.'

'Can we get a boat through?' asked Holmes.

'I would imagine so, sir. There is still a right of way for canal boats, though we do not see so many since the railway came.'

Holmes was rubbing his hands. 'This is excellent!' he exclaimed. 'Lord Backwater, will you be good enough to summon Inspector Scott so that we may make our plans?'

'You are not planning an attack tonight?' I asked.

'No, Watson, to attack in darkness would merely give our opponents an advantage. We can lay our plans tonight and, with any luck, come upon them from two directions when they are least prepared, at dawn.'

Word was sent to Inspector Scott and, once he had arrived, a council of war gathered in the library, numbered among which was the imperturbable Arnold.

Under my friend's direction a plan was constructed, whereby Inspector Scott would bring a party of police officers down the West Tunnel before daybreak to be in position before dawn. In the meantime a landward party composed of Lord Backwater, Holmes and myself and guided by Arnold would advance under cover of darkness to overwhelm any outside guard and seize the entrance to the ice-house.

'Are you sure my sister will come to no harm by our attack?' asked Lord Backwater.

'They seem to be only two, to guard the two entrances to the ice-house,' said Holmes. 'If they are taking proper care they should be one at each end. If so, Scott's party can take the inner guard while we deal with the outer. If they are careless enough to be both at one end then we must make sure that neither escapes within to harm Lady Patricia.'

Inspector Scott went off to organise his part of the arrangements, while the rest of us passed the night around the library table, waiting for the clock to tell us that it was time to be about our business.

At last Holmes indicated that the time had come. Buttoning up our coats and taking our weapons we clambered into the carriage that was to be driven by young Tommy. Catherine, too, had been made a part of our company, ready to assist her lady when we had freed her.

We went north from the Hall, until we could dimly see the glimmer of the canal away to our right. 'Now,' said Holmes, 'we leave our transport here. Tommy, stay here and look after Catherine until you hear my whistle, then make towards the tunnel mouth until you see us. The rest of the way we go on foot, gentlemen, and we must be in place while it is still dark.'

'Yes, sir. Good luck, sir,' said Tommy, and jumping down we set off at a brisk pace with Arnold in the lead. We began to mount the long rise above the canal tunnel and eventually Arnold turned and whispered, 'There it is, Mr Holmes, the cedar tree that was by the entrance to the ice-house.'

'Well done,' said Holmes. 'Where does the entrance lie in relation to the tree?'

'Directly down the slope, sir, about two yards in front of the tree.'

'Excellent,' said Holmes. 'We shall make a detour, gentlemen. We shall go up this side of the slope and come down behind that cedar by a roundabout route and in total silence, please, gentlemen.'

Now Sherlock Holmes took the lead as we made our way up the rise and turned down again towards the cedar tree. About ten feet from the tree Holmes crouched in the long grass. He drew out his watch and turned its face to the dim light of the sky.

'We have a little while to wait before the sky lightens,' he whispered. 'Lord Backwater, you and Arnold should stay here and keep down. Watson and I will move down to this side of the tree. When you see us move, follow up, hard.'

Our companions nodded their understanding and Holmes began to wriggle away through the grass towards the tree with me a short distance behind him. Very soon we were in position, side by side behind the trunk, each able to see around our side of the tree.

Time passed as slowly as it always does when one is tensed and expectant of action, but eventually the sky began to lighten and soon we heard a mutter of voices below us. Holmes stole a quick glance at his watch.

'We must hope Scott is in place,' he whispered. 'Be ready, Watson.'

I had raised myself to a crouch, easing my stiff leg, and laid my hand on the revolver in my pocket, when two dark figures emerged seemingly out of the very ground in front of us. They stepped a few feet down the slope and it was apparent that they were about to ease themselves.

'Both of them!' Holmes hissed. 'Now, Watson!' and he launched himself around the tree and down the slope.

I sprang away at the same moment, and took the righthand man below the knees with as neat a tackle as the Old Deer Park at Richmond ever saw. He went down like a log, but I had not knocked all the fight out of him and we had quite a vigorous struggle before I was able to put the muzzle of my Adams under his jaw and convince him to lie still while I handcuffed him.

As soon as I had done so I looked around for Holmes, but there was no sign of him. I found the steps in the grass that led down to the ice-house and tumbled down them and through the rotted wooden door at the bottom. In the first chamber I found Lord Backwater with his sister, still in her groom's clothing, in his arms, and I went through the archway towards a lantern's light.

In the second chamber I found Holmes, Inspector Scott and three constables standing around a figure on the ground. It was the bearded ruffian I had seen at the bridge.

'We have lost one of them, Watson,' said Holmes as I entered. 'He was a fraction too quick for me above ground and got away down the steps. I followed, fearing he meant harm to Lady Patricia, but he was intent on escaping if he could. The Inspector and his men had landed from the tunnel and he ran headlong into them. One of them, I am afraid, was a little too quick on the trigger.'

'Never mind,' I said. 'Lady Patricia is safe and I have the other blackguard trussed up outside.'

We made our way outside and, as Holmes whistled for our driver, I looked around for my prisoner. To my astonishment there was no sign of him.

'He has gone, Holmes!' I exclaimed in bewilderment.

'He cannot have gone far,' he remarked, 'and there is his trail.'

He pointed and I could see that, from the flattened area where we had rolled and fought, a dark trail led downhill through the dewy grass. We followed it across the slope to the lip of the canal tunnel, where it ended abruptly. Beneath the parapet was a wide pool, so that boats could swing around there or wait their turn through the tunnel. The sodden shape of our quarry floated face down in the middle of the pool.

'But he could not have swum in handcuffs!' I expostulated.

'No more he could,' said Holmes grimly. 'But the Ring induced fierce discipline in its members. He was undoubtedly unwilling to be questioned let alone hung for the murders of Lord Backwater and old Williams,' and he turned away.

Despite the loss of our prisoners it was a self-congratulatory party that returned to Backwater Hall and, if there is such a feast as a celebratory breakfast, that is what we enjoyed. Arnold vanished as soon as we got back, to reappear formally clad and serving an enormous breakfast with a wide smile on his usually expressionless countenance.

The long night and a heavy breakfast sent most of us to our beds and it was later than usual when we gathered for luncheon. Lady Patricia, under Catherine's care, looked entirely recovered from her ordeal and thanked Holmes prettily for his efforts on her behalf.

Her brother, too, was warmly congratulatory. 'If we have not seen eye to eye on occasions, Mr Holmes, it was entirely because I did not understand the subtleties of your methods. Now I can only say that I do not know how to express my gratitude to you. Not only have you avenged the murder of my father, but you have saved my sister. I cannot thank you enough.'

Holmes beamed, as he always did in the light of honest admiration, but he raised a warning hand. 'I am, of course, pleased that I have been able to solve the mystery in which you first consulted me, Lord Backwater, but in doing so we have uncovered only a part of the mystery that lay behind your father's death. The Ring believes that you hold something on which it has a claim. Until that matter is revealed, you and your family will remain in danger of the Ring's machinations.'

'But how can we find out what it is they want?' asked Lord Patrick. 'For all I know it may be something that, for the safety of my house, I would be willing to give them.'

'You would be most unwise to do so,' said Holmes. 'Besides, we do know that the Ring's attention seems to be fastened on the Black Queen, whatever that may be, and you have your father's instructions as to that fund.'

'The Black Queen account does not, by a long chalk, outweigh the funds which I inherited, Mr Holmes. If I knew what they wanted I might easily pay them.'

'You would never be free of them,' said Holmes. 'Already they have taken a sizeable sum from you and were, no doubt, planning another demand. No, Lord Backwater, we must find the significance of that account, the reasons why the Ring claims it and, most of all, the person who has directed their attempts here.'

'And how will we do that?' our host asked.

'I have every hope that I shall soon receive word from someone who can explain at least two of those things to us. If that is correct, then I may well be able to answer the third. Until that time, Dr Watson and I will, if we may, remain at Backwater.'

'Of course, Mr Holmes, stay as long as you wish. Indeed, if we are, as you say, in continuing danger from the Ring, then I urge you to remain until the danger is past.'

Nineteen

❦

A Fatal Suspicion

Midway through the following morning Holmes and I were in the library when Arnold appeared.

'Excuse me, Mr Holmes,' he said, 'but were you aware of Inspector Scott's presence at the Hall today?'

'No, Arnold,' said Holmes, 'I cannot say that I am, and am sure he would have sought me out if he had been here. Why do you ask?'

'There is a constable at the door, sir. He says that he understood the Inspector to be here, sir.'

'There must be some mistake,' said Holmes. 'I will have a word with him,' and laying down his newspaper he rose and followed Arnold into the hall while I followed suit.

The officer in the hall was the young constable we had met in the beech glade on our first arrival in Backwater.

'Good morning, Mr Holmes, Doctor.'

'I understand,' said Holmes, 'that you believe your Inspector to have called here his morning.'

'To be precise, sir, I know Inspector Scott to have called here,' said the young officer. 'I was to take the trap to the railway station to collect Superintendent Thorpe. Inspector Scott had me bring him to the back of the beech glade. He said he would walk down through the woods to the Hall and I was to pick him up in two hours.'

Holmes' eyes narrowed. 'Do you know why the Inspector intended to call on me?' he asked.

'He said he was delivering some photographs, sir, and there was something he wished to discuss.'

'And what time was it when you left him at the far end of the beech glade?' asked Holmes.

The constable drew out his watch. 'Exactly two hours and five minutes ago, sir.'

Holmes' mouth had drawn itself into a thin line. 'I do not like this,' he said, and strode across the hall into the small drawing-room that lay behind. Without pausing he marched out through the french windows on to the terrace and stood, gazing across the park to the entrance of the beech wood. Nothing moved in the sunlit landscape.

'It should have taken him no more then twenty minutes to drop down through the beech glade and across the park,' said Holmes. 'Something is amiss.'

He spun towards the constable. 'Officer, kindly bring your trap around to the terrace and convey us to the beech glade.'

'Do you think something has happened to the Inspector, Mr Holmes?'

'Yes,' said Holmes shortly. 'Now let us see what it is that has delayed him.'

The constable ran back through the house and soon had his trap by the terrace. As we pulled away from the house he whipped up his horse and we reached the edge of the woods in no time. Rolling through the patches of light and shade under the great trees Holmes and I looked all around us for any indication of the police officer's whereabouts.

We were about half-way along the stand of trees when Holmes shouted, 'There! Stop, constable!' and pointed.

Ahead of us lay a bright patch of ground where the sun splashed down through the green canopy, and at its heart lay a still, dark shape.

The constable pulled his horse up and Holmes and I were out of the trap and running almost before the wheels had stopped, the officer jogging behind.

At the centre of the brightly lit patch of ground lay the Inspector. He was face down with his arms outstretched, his face turned to the left and his knees slightly flexed. It was immediately apparent that he was dead, the cause of death being a single bullet that had struck him in the back of the skull and passed through his head to leave above the left eyebrow.

'Inspector Scott!' exclaimed the young constable. 'Is he dead, Doctor?'

'I am afraid so,' I said.

'Constable,' said Holmes, 'Inspector Scott was very proud of you. Now remember how he trained you. Take the trap and fetch your Superintendent at once. Watson and I will guard this scene until you return.'

As the officer left Holmes smote his right fist into his left palm. 'Shot down like a dog!' he exclaimed. 'I should have been able to prevent this, Watson.'

He began to pace around the area, closely examining the ground and the tree trunks in the vicinity. At last he called me to him as he stood by a tree a few yards from the body.

'Look here, Watson,' and he pointed to a tiny, blazed mark on the trunk, a little above his head. 'There is where the spent bullet clipped this tree after hitting Scott.'

He turned and looked across the spot where the body lay. 'We may, I think, take an approximate line from this point which should limit our area of enquiry,' and he stepped away, passing close to the dead man's head.

He entered the low scrub that surrounded the glade and, after a moment, called me again.

'See,' he said, pointing with his stick as I joined him. 'Here are the marks where a tall man in well-made shoes has crouched behind these bushes, waiting for Scott to step innocently into that sunlit clearing.'

'But why was he shot?' I asked.

'For the photographs, I imagine,' said Holmes, and walked back to the body. He knelt beside the dead man and carefully felt in each of his pockets. 'Hullo!' he exclaimed suddenly. 'What have we here?'

He straightened up, holding a brown envelope that he had drawn from Scott's tunic pocket. It was unsealed and he lifted the flap.

'No, Watson, I was wrong. It was not for the photographs, for here they are.'

He passed them to me. There were three large prints, two showing the tumbled interior of Williams' shack and a third which was a close-up of the blood-marks on the back of the violin.

'Perhaps there was no opportunity to take them,' I suggested.

'Nonsense,' said Holmes. 'If the killer had been disturbed by somebody passing this way, the body would have been discovered. They did not take the photographs because they did not know about them or because they did not care about them. So why on earth was he killed?'

The trap returned, bringing a party of constables and Superintendent Thorpe. The Superintendent introduced himself to us.

'This is a grim business, Mr Holmes. Ian Scott was one of our brightest Inspectors and a personal friend of mine. Have you reached any conclusions?'

Holmes led him around the scene and showed him how the Inspector had been ambushed.

'And you believe this to be connected with the killing of Lord Backwater and old Williams?' said the Superintendent.

'I should be very surprised if it were not,' said Holmes. 'I have always found coincidence an uneasy guest.'

'But, as I recall, Lord Backwater and Williams were bludgeoned. Scott was shot by what seems to have been a sporting rifle,' said the Superintendent.

'You are familiar with the facts of those cases?' asked Holmes.

'In the main,' said Thorpe. 'Scott reported to me as well as to Colonel Caddage. I understand that Lord Backwater was the victim, not of poachers as the Colonel would have it, but of thugs who were members of that vile society that calls itself the Ring, of which Williams was also a member.'

'Quite,' said Holmes. 'At first the Ring operated through members like Williams and two bullies who were imported into this area. Their chosen weapon was the cudgel. But recent events have deprived their master of their services. Now he is forced, perhaps, to do his own dirty work. If poor Scott's death has achieved nothing else, it has forced our man further into the open.'

He gazed bitterly back towards the dead man. We followed his gaze.

'Why do you believe he was killed, Mr Holmes?' asked Thorpe.

'I have been asking myself that question,' said my friend. 'You know that he was on his way to deliver some photographs to me? At first I thought he had been ambushed to prevent me seeing those pictures, but he still had them on his person. I have them here. I cannot, at present, imagine why he died. When did you last see him?'

'Only last night,' said Thorpe. 'He was leaving the Colonel's as I was arriving. We exchanged a few words. He told me that he would bring you your photographs this morning and he said he had an idea who was behind it all. He said that when he saw you he wanted to check something with Dr Watson.'

'With Watson!' echoed Holmes, and arched an eyebrow.

'It sounds', I said, 'as if he wanted to check my recollection of some detail of old Williams' death.'

'I dare say that was his reason,' said Holmes. 'Come, Watson, there is nothing more we can do here. Superintendent, I must think hard about this latest development. When I have done so I shall let you have my conclusions.'

'I shall welcome them, Mr Holmes. Good day to you both.'

We left on foot and Holmes was silent all the way back to the Hall. Arnold had apprised Lord Backwater of our hurried departure and he had held back luncheon for us. Now he was anxious for our news and, over the dining-table, Holmes described the second tragedy in the beech glade. Like us he could think of no reason for the murder of the Inspector, but we did not have long to contemplate it for, as the meal was ending, there was an interruption.

Arnold entered with his bland features looking positively puzzled.

'Forgive me, My Lord,' he said, 'but there is a person at the door who will give no name. He says only that he has come from London in answer to your advertisements.'

'My advertisements!' ejaculated Lord Patrick.

'Pardon me, Lord Backwater,' interjected Holmes, 'but I have been expecting such a development. Can we have this man in?'

'Very well, Mr Holmes, if you wish it. Arnold, show the gentleman into the library and serve coffee there. We shall join him very shortly.'

As Arnold left, Lord Backwater looked at Holmes. 'You had been expecting him?' he asked.

'Since hearing your father's narrative, Lord Backwater, I have been anxious to locate the one person who I believe can explain to us many things that are impenetrable at present. I hope that this is he.'

'Then let us see him,' said Lord Patrick, and we rose together.

As we entered the library a tall man raised himself from a seat by the window. 'Good day,' he said. 'May I ask which of you is Lord Backwater?'

'I have that honour,' said Lord Patrick. 'Whom have I the honour of addressing?'

'I,' said the stranger, 'am the Man from the Gates of Hell.'

Twenty

THE MAN FROM THE GATES OF HELL

The man who stood before the sunlit window was as tall as Holmes, with fair hair turning silver. His face bore the deep and even tan of one who has been long abroad. In his hand he held a wide-brimmed soft hat and his clothes were of an American, rather than an English, cut.

Lord Backwater darted forward and clasped the stranger's hand. 'In my late father's name and my own I bid you welcome, sir! But what was this about my advertisement?'

'If the gentleman will be kind enough to give us his name,' said Holmes, 'I can explain the advertisement.'

The fair man looked questioningly at Holmes.

'This is Mr Sherlock Holmes, the consulting detective,' said Lord Backwater, 'and this is his associate, Dr Watson. They have been dealing with my father's death and certain other events which seem to have arisen from it.'

The stranger nodded to each of us and drew a slip of newsprint from his pocket. 'My name,' he said, 'is Peter Collins, and I came in answer to this advertisement, which seems to have appeared in every London newspaper.'

'"The Gates of Hell. Peter Collins must contact Lord B to break the Ring,"' recited Holmes. 'If our visitor will give us his true name I shall explain the reason for that advertisement.'

'What the deuce is going on here?' demanded Lord Backwater. 'You say that Peter Collins is not this man's true name?'

'I suggest, Lord Backwater, that if you were to assure your guest that anything he tells us will remain a secret, he may be willing to confirm his identity and tell us a great deal more,' said Holmes.

'That is, of course, the case,' said Lord Patrick. 'I do not know who you are, sir, but I have every reason to believe that my father trusted you. For that reason you may trust me and all of us here.'

'What makes you believe my name is not Peter Collins?' the stranger asked Holmes.

My friend had seated himself and now poured himself some coffee. 'Because I know it to be Patrick Connors.'

The tall man lowered himself into his chair, his eyes never leaving Holmes' face.

'You seem to know so much about me that perhaps you can tell it better than I,' he said.

'That may well be true, up to a point,' said Holmes, 'but beyond that point you must assist me. Now, let me see.'

He steepled his fingers in front of his face as he marshalled his facts, then looked up.

'You are Patrick Connors, who was adopted at an early age by a couple called Keep, the shoemaker and his wife of this village. They raised you alongside another orphan boy called James Loveridge.'

Both Lord Backwater and I interrupted. 'But Holmes! That boy died on Eaglehawk Neck. We know he did.'

Holmes continued, unperturbed, 'For reasons we know about, and through the dishonesty of Rupert Varley, you and your foster-brother were transported to Van Diemen's Land. There you attempted a joint escape from Point Puer. James Loveridge succeeded but you failed. What happened to you after that I know not. James Loveridge concealed his identity, acquired great wealth and rose to a position of honour and public affection in this country. For most of that time he believed you to have died at Eaglehawk Neck – until, that is, you made contact with him recently. At some point you entrusted your boyhood friend with a very large sum of money, money which it appears is claimed by the organisation calling itself the Ring. Because of their purported claim against you, the Ring had you watched and set an ambush for you when next you visited Backwater. Unluckily, that ambush resulted in the death of Lord Backwater, after which you retreated to London. That is really all that I know of you.'

Collins or Connors continued to gaze at my friend with level blue eyes.

'How did you come by my name?' he asked at last.

Holmes smiled. 'When I first realised that the late Lord Backwater had been connected with this place in his youth, I sought the assistance of the landlord of the Backwater Arms. He could recall James Loveridge, but he was only able to give me your surname. Nevertheless, I knew that you had employed the pseudonym 'Peter Collins' on your visits to Backwater and I had seen the initials J. L. and P. C cut more than once into the trunk of the beech tree that was your boyhood rendezvous and the scene of Lord Backwater's death – "the old place" – so it seemed reasonable that your forename began with "P". No Protestant Englishman would christen his son and daughter Patrick and Patricia unless he had some reason. I believed that Lord Backwater's children were named in memory of his foster-brother. The landlord also told me that "Peter Collins" visited from London, which led me to place my advertisements there.'

'But how did you realise that the Man from the Gates of Hell was Lord Backwater's foster-brother?' I asked. 'We heard the description of his death in Van Diemen's Land!'

'We heard,' said Holmes, 'a narrative which set out at its beginning the fact that Lord Backwater would not break an obligation of confidence to someone. Did it not strike you as singular that, throughout his manuscript, Lord Backwater never once named his beloved foster-brother? I have always believed that the absence of what should be present is as important as the presence of what should not be, hence I concluded that the foster-brother had somehow survived on Eaglehawk Neck and Lord Backwater had come to know it. When the evidence indicates that the impossible has happened then whatever flows from it is also possible. *Ergo*, the Man from the Gates of Hell must be Patrick Connors.'

'Astonishing!' said Lord Backwater and Connors grinned ruefully. 'So you smoked me out, Mr Holmes,' he said. 'Now what can I do for you?'

'You were present when Lord Backwater was attacked and killed by the Ring's ruffians,' said Holmes, 'but you may not be aware that there have been two more deaths since – an old wretch who guided the murderers to the beech glade and, this very day, a police inspector. It is evident that the shedding of blood will go on unless we can reveal the man who is directing the Ring's operations. To do that we need to know why the Ring believes it has a claim on you and Lord Backwater.'

Connors passed a hand over his face. 'You know the story as far as Eaglehawk Neck?' he asked.

'Yes,' replied Holmes, 'and other than your membership of the Ring, there is no clue there.'

'When I lay on the Neck with a hole in my shoulder pouring blood on to the shells and that ravenous dog slavering at my throat, I can imagine why Jim thought I was dead, for I thought I was a goner. I heard the guards shouting and then everything went black.'

He paused. 'I awoke in the infirmary at Port Arthur, but I still believed I would die and I took no interest in what passed around me. I clung to the knowledge that I had seen Jim on the other side of the fence and, as day after day went by and he wasn't brought back, I knew that I'd got him away and prayed that he would survive the bush and find a way out of Van Diemen's Land. Slowly I got better, and they questioned me about Jim. I told them that Jim had run into the water and tried to swim around the fence. His bloodstained trousers had washed up on the beach so they believed the sharks had got him and they didn't look for him.'

He paused again. 'Somehow they patched me back together,' he went on, 'and one day I managed to get up and walk. That day I asked one of the screws what would happen to me. He laughed and said, "There's no doubt where you're going – to Sydney to be hanged."'

Twenty-One

THE OLD HELL

'When we fled from Point Puer,' he continued, 'I believed I had killed Hunter. Unfortunately that was not true. His head was so hard that I had only brained him. Still, he was now wandering about Point Puer like a bewildered ox, his wits completely gone, and I had the satisfaction of knowing that his life as a bully was ended. Nevertheless, attempted murder of a screw and a prison break were quite enough to hang me.'

A slight smile lit his features. 'But that was not to be. Hunter with his addled wits could never testify against me and the boys of the Ring were agreed that, if they were taken to Sydney, they would swear that I struck Hunter in defence of my foster-brother. The Commandant saw no point in sending all of us to Sydney for a trial that might end with my acquittal and might give us all the chance of an escape. So I was dealt with at Port Arthur. I was charged with striking a lawful officer and breaking gaol. Seven years was added to my sentence and I was sent to Norfolk Island. Do you know where Norfolk Island lies?'

'About a thousand miles east of Australia's mainland,' said Holmes.

'That's right. A thousand miles from anywhere. It is — or it was — one of the most beautiful spots on the face of the earth, with pine-clad hills, lush vegetation, flowers of jasmine, sugarcane, figs, lemons. It might have been a paradise if we had not turned it into Hell.'

He gazed out of the window, and I guessed that he was looking down a longer vista than the lawns of Backwater Hall.

'Every stage of the System,' he went on, 'the county gaols, the hulks, the transport ships, Botany Bay, Port Macquarie, Port Arthur, each of these is a step, a step downwards and further into the System's maw. If the System was Hell, Norfolk Island was the deepest of its pits. There they sent the untameable, the irreducibly vicious, the insane and the desperately rebellious, to rot for ever. To guard us they sent the worst men, often no better than the convicts, mad, corrupt and brutal. Nothing that they did ever came under review. Sydney was a thousand miles away and England sixteen thousand miles further. There I was sent to survive thirteen years if I could.

'My tattoos from Point Puer stood me in good stead. Norfolk Island was the birthplace and capital of the Ring, and there they recognised no authority but their own, but the marks showed them I was a likely recruit and I was soon made welcome in the Ring itself.

'All business at Norfolk Island was controlled by the Ring, for it numbered among its Brothers not only convicts and guards but even officers of the garrison. Once I was one of them my life became a lot easier.

'I might have done as others were doing, and used my membership of the Ring to ease the passing of the years until time wore out my sentence, but I looked at the wretched old crawlers about me, men who had come there in their youth and stayed to rot, and knew that I must never become like them. They would tell newcomers that the way to go on was to take one day at a time, to see no further ahead than next Sunday, but I knew that if I did that I should realise one day that all my youth had been lost, one day at a time. Even for a member of the Ring it was easy to have years added to your sentence for some imagined infraction of the rules and proverb said that those who came to Norfolk Island never went back. So desperate were some that they drew lots to murder each other, both of the parties being thus freed – one by his partner's hand and the other by a government rope in Sydney. I knew that I must find my own way out.

'With that in mind I set out to be as useful a member of the Ring as I might, for I knew there was no chance of escaping without the Brotherhood's assistance. Among the military officers who joined the Ring was a young Lieutenant who taught the organisation a valuable trick as it seemed. The Ring had great power within the island, often deciding who should live or die, but it operated solely through its sworn members, for it lacked the freedom that money would give it, the freedom to bribe those outside its ranks. This officer was well hated and feared by both soldiers and convicts, but he wielded great power for a particular reason.

'He had begun a system of taxation upon the ships that called there, taking fees from masters to discharge their cargoes at the island. Those who would not pay found that there were insurmountable obstacles to the purchase of their goods by the garrison and soon every vessel was paying his commission. A proportion of his collection he passed on to the Ring. In the first place it enabled us to swell our store of tobacco, rum and foodstuffs, but it also meant that our power over the island was greatly increased. Now guards who were not Brothers could be persuaded to turn a blind eye to the Ring's transactions and witnesses could be purchased to speak for the Ring, the more believable since the authorities knew fairly well who was of the Ring and who was not.

'Every day I sought to learn all that I could about the island and its systems and every night I lay and pondered the possibilities of escape.

The cliffs that surrounded the island were an insurmountable obstacle, and the few landing places were heavily guarded. At Kingston, where goods were landed, ships did not come alongside, but lay off while they were unloaded by small boats. I was beginning to believe that my task was hopeless, but Fortune is a strange lady. I have known her hard and I have known her gentle and I have known her wear some strange disguises.

'She came to my hammock one night, in the guise of a soldier with an order to go at once to the Lieutenant's quarters. I had done him many errands and such a summons was not unusual. The Lieutenant occupied one of a row of cottages at the edge of Kingston. I followed his messenger to the officer's cottage, the door of which stood open to the warm night, lamplight spilling out. The soldier left me there and I entered cautiously.

'The Lieutenant was drunk in some degree. He sprawled behind his desk in waistcoat and shirt-sleeves with a glass in his hand.

'"You," he accused me, "are planning to escape."

'I stammered a denial, but he said, "Don't anger me by lying, Connors. I've seen you prowling the island like a cat, sniffing into every corner. You tried it at Port Arthur and you're looking to try it again here."

'"There's no denying that I'd far rather go than stay, sir," I answered.

'"For all your prying and seeking you'll find no way," said the Lieutenant, and he leaned across the table, grinning at me. "There's only one way off Norfolk Island, boy. D'ye know what that is?"

'"No, sir," I said nervously, for his drunkenness and the topic of his conversation puzzled me.

'"The only way," he said, "is by a Yankee boat. English skippers daren't take you, Frogs won't, but a Yankee'll do it for money. But then, you haven't got any money, have you, Connors?"

"'No, sir'" I said again.

"He gulped his drink noisily and peered at me through narrowed eyes. 'You can climb like a cat, can't ye?" he demanded.

"'Yes, I can climb, sir," I said.

"'Could you climb that chimney?" he asked, jerking a thumb at the fireplace behind him.

'I stepped into the empty fireplace, crouched and looked up. The chimney of the wooden cottage was made of rough-hewn stone. As I looked up I could see a square of starlit sky above.

"'I don't see why not," I said.

"'Good!" he ejaculated. "Come with me!" and lurching to his feet he led me out of the cottage. He took me to the front door of the next house. A light shone inside but there was no sound. I knew this cottage to be the billet of another officer, Lieutenant Dawson.

"'Lieutenant Dawson—' I began, but he hissed at me, "Dawson won't bother us," and, taking a key from his pocket, he unlocked the door. As I followed him in I saw that Dawson sat sprawled back in a wooden armchair with his back to the door. In front of him a low lamp burned on a table littered with cards, bottles and two glasses. I thought him senselessly drunk until I walked around the table.

"'He's dead, sir!" I cried, for now I could see that Dawson wore a look of surprise on his face and his left hand clutched the breast of his waistcoat where blood had spilled and darkened.

"'Dead enough," said the Lieutenant. "My brother officer and I were playing cards when we had a falling out. The fool drew his little pistol on me and when I tried to take it from him it went off."

'Frightened as I now was, I could tell that was a lie, for there was no powder burn on Dawson's waistcoat and the pistol lay on the far side of the table, but I kept my opinions to myself.

'"Now, this is all a damnable embarrassment to me," said the Lieutenant, "so we're going to act like Brothers of the Ring. First you shall help me, then I shall help you."

'"How can I help you, sir?" I asked.

'"First we shall arrange things so that it seems that Dawson sat on alone after our game, when I had gone. Then we shall make it seem that he took his own life with the pistol. Come, put the shutters up and bar them!"

'I closed the shutters while he rearranged the scene at the table, stowing the cards in a drawer and removing one glass. Next he placed the little pistol on the floor below Dawson's right hand.

'I watched in puzzlement, not seeing the part I was to play. "Now," he said, "I shall leave. You must take this key and lock the door from the inside. Leave the key in the lock and climb out by the chimney. When Dawson's servant arrives from the barracks in the morning he will see that his master shot himself while locked in and alone.'

'It was a cunning plan but I saw a drawback. "When I go up the chimney I shall knock down soot. They will know in the morning that someone went out the chimney."

'"So they will," he agreed, 'though they will know 'twas not me. Still, you are right."

'He started to take papers and letters from Dawson's drawers, crumpling them and piling them in the fireplace. When there was a little mound of them he handed me a piece of paper and a tinderbox. "Take these up with you," he said, "and at the top set alight to the paper and drop it into the hearth. The fire will cover any soot that falls. They will merely believe that Dawson was destroying papers before he killed himself."

'We proceeded according to his plan and, in a very few minutes, I was at the chimney top. My burning paper soon fired those below and

I clambered down the rough-laid exterior of the chimney to where the Lieutenant waited for me.

'"Well done, boy," he said. "Now, so we have no misunderstanding, repeat to me the Oath of the Ring."

'I did so and he looked me long in the face. Then he said, "And do you wholly acknowledge the Ring's law – that any favour shown you will repay?"

'"Of course," I said.

'"Then come with me," he commanded and I followed him away from the cottages and down to the beach, where he jumped into a boat.

'"Row," he commanded me, "as though your life depended on it, for I assure you that it does," and with my heart pounding with hope and excitement I took up the oars.

'There were no jetties or wharves at Kingston. As I have already mentioned, ships stood out and were unloaded by boat. As we pulled further out I could see three vessels lying at anchor, but two of them I knew to be British.

'At the Lieutenant's instruction I pulled alongside the third ship and we clambered aboard, where a word from the Lieutenant sent a seaman for his skipper. What passed between them I do not know, for it was done in the captain's cabin. When the Lieutenant returned to the deck he looked me over again.

'"I have done my best for you, Connors," he said, "and it has cost a pretty penny to persuade the good captain to sail early. As of this moment you are the ship's boy of the *Juliet Jones*, and a citizen of the United States. Whatever you become you will always be a Brother of the Ring and you owe the Ring one hundred pounds. Never forget that you also owe the Brotherhood for your freedom, and never forget that if you are found on British soil, on a British vessel or in British waters and identified you will hang, American or not. I wish you good luck, boy!"

'With that he was over the side and gone and I stood alone on the deck, hardly able to believe my change in fortune. It was growing light as the *Juliet Jones* weighed anchor. Once away from the land the morning breeze filled her sails and blew on the face of her new ship's boy, Peter Collins, like the very breath of freedom as he stood on her deck and watched the hills of Norfolk Island sink into the ocean.'

Twenty-Two

THE BLACK QUEEN OF TUMUROA

Lord Backwater's guest paused again and gazed out of the window. I was struck by that even, expressionless look on his face that I have seen before on those who have been long in prison. It comes from using the face as a mask so that no warder or official may read a man's intentions or feelings in his expression.

'I was not yet sixteen years of age,' he said, almost as though talking to himself. 'I had been taken from home and flung down all those steps to the blackest pit of the System and by the most unimaginable chance I had survived and was free.

'Can you imagine, gentlemen,' he said, turning to us, 'what that felt like?' and we shook our heads for truly we could not.

'The skipper of the *Juliet Jones* found me a willing worker and kept me aboard as he cruised among the islands of the Pacific and for two years I lived the carefree life of a young sailor among the sweetest places and the most gentle people on earth.

'At last the skipper grew homesick for America but I was besotted by the islands and wished to stay, so he paid me off and left me on Tumuroa.

'There were more white men in the islands in those days than you might think. Some were bolters like me, out of the penal colonies on foreign ships. Some were seamen, again like me, who could not bear to leave what seemed like paradise on earth. Food was all around us, drink was there when we wanted it and the lovely girls of the islands thought it an honour to be partner to a white man. So I passed more than a year in idle contentment until I almost believed that the iron of Point Puer and Norfolk Island had washed out of my blood.

'But it was not, in the end, the life for me. I began to see what happened to those who stayed too long. They became weathered old wrecks of men, given over completely to drink and rambling endlessly about the homes that they had left so many years and so many miles away. So it came to me that I must be doing something that had some purpose.

'On Tumuroa the natives fished for pearls. They would go out in their little craft and send divers down, but not in fancy dress with air pumped to them. They would fill their lungs and take a great rock and leap over the side, letting the weight of the rock carry them to the seabed as quickly as possible. There, while their breath held, they would scrabble to fill a bag with shells and bring it back up with them.

'I have always enjoyed athletic activity and, at first, I went out in their boats and matched my ability against theirs purely as a sport, but very soon I realised the considerable strength and skill they employed and the deadly danger of their task. As I became more proficient, I realised as well that here was a source of income.

'I became, in a while, a moderately effective diver, and began to accumulate funds from my operations. As soon as I was able I sent a draft to the Lieutenant, paying off my debt to the Ring and, I thought, freeing me from its Brotherhood. I knew not whether he was still at Norfolk Island, but I knew that my unsigned letter would follow him to whatever posting he had taken. On the day I committed that draft to the post I poured acid over my own arms to remove for ever the Ring's signs.'

He paused, and drew a deep breath, as though the action still gave him satisfaction.

'Freed of any obligations, save to myself, I worked at pearling until, by careful dealing, I had accumulated a decent sum. Now I became anxious to be on my way. The attractions of the islands remained, but there was nothing there for me to do and I had grown up in my time there; grown up to realise that I could not let my time pass meaninglessly.

'Fate turned to me again, for out of one of the last harvests of shell I brought ashore came one, large, flawless black pearl.'

'The Black Queen of Tumuroa,' said Holmes.

'You have heard of it?' asked Connors.

'I should have remembered it before,' said my friend. 'Precious jewels are the focus, if not the cause, of so much crime, that it behoves a detective to know all that he can of them. Is it not now in the collection of one of the Czar's family?'

'It is, I believe,' said Connors, 'and how right you are. When I first saw the Black Queen I knew at once that I held a fortune in my hand. I should, perhaps, have realised that I also held in my hand a magnet that would draw death around me.

'I left the islands and took my accumulation, topped now by that magnificent black pearl, to Hong Kong. There I had no trouble in disposing of my collection at a sensible price. At last I believed that the convict boy from Norfolk Island could be forgotten. I had sufficient funds to make me more than wealthy anywhere in the world.

'That delusion lasted me only hours. During the night after I had sold the Black Queen a message was slipped under the door of my hotel room. I can recall it word for word. It said, "Connors, you are free because the Ring made you so. If you would stay free the Ring must have a half-share in your good fortune," and it bore the Ring's emblems.

'When I first held the Black Queen I believed that it had closed the past behind me for ever, but now that note had opened it all again. I felt the tattooed hands of the Ring reaching out to drag me back to Hell. I fled from Hong Kong the next day, for I dared not stay a moment longer on British soil, and made my way to California.

'For a short while I felt safe there. I was not on English soil. But there are many Australians in California and I had not been there long before I received another message from the Ring.

'I might, I suppose, have paid them, but I felt that to do so would only guarantee that they would bleed me dry. So I ran again. And kept running.'

For once the passive face twisted in bitter reflection. 'Oh how I ran,' he said. 'For more years than I can recall I went wherever the next boat or train would take me – India, Ceylon, Egypt, who knows where – and each time they found me, till at last I fetched up in South America. From there I went north into Mexico and I seemed to have left them behind. I crossed into Texas and there I stayed. Slowly the years mounted with no sign of the Ring. I began to breathe freely again. At last I could enjoy the profits of the Black Queen. I bought myself what they call a "spread" and there I raised horses.

'All the time I watched and listened for any sign of the Ring, but none came. I heard how New South Wales and Van Diemen's Land were no longer convict colonies, then Western Australia and Norfolk Island had closed. When I knew that Norfolk Island was gone I surmised that the Ring must have died. I waited a few years more and then I slipped back to England.

'Nothing could have kept me from Backwater. I had been a hunted exile so long that there was a deep longing in me to see my childhood home. I had no fear of being recognised, for I had been gone for forty years.

'So I came home. I do not know what might have been the conclusion if Rupert Varley had been alive, but they told me that he had met a better end than he deserved. I went to the churchyard and there I found that someone had raised a handsome stone over my good old Uncle Joe and Aunt Lisa. When they told me at the inn that it was a whim of the new Lord Backwater a strange idea came to me. If someone had done to our foster-parents' grave what I would have done, and done it in secret, I wondered if that could possibly be Jim.

'I sent a note to the Hall, a note signed only "The Man from Hell", to meet me at the old place. Can you imagine how we greeted each other by that old tree? We were two of the richest men in England and we stood beneath the old beech and wept like the children we had been when last we stood there.

'Together we made our plans, that I should make doubly sure that the Ring had given up its claim on me, and then I should settle here in Backwater. In the meantime I transferred most of my funds to Jim, to do with as his own and to help those that he helped.

'I came again and each time I was careful. I would stay a day or two at the Backwater Arms, being just a holiday-maker in the country. On the last day I would send a note to Jim, take my bags to the station and then slip back through the woods to the beech glade and meet him. The last time we met was, indeed, to have been the last. I was satisfied that the Ring had forgotten me and I was going to move to Backwater.

'When we were attacked I recognised the ruffians who did it. There was the mad old fiddler from the Backwater Arms and two more I had seen with him at the pub. Jim fought like a lion and kept telling me to run, but I could not. Then, when he was struck down and I could see he was killed, there was nothing more to do except run.'

He paused again, far longer this time. 'We had survived it all, Van Diemen's Land, Norfolk Island, all our wanderings, and we had come back home to be two old men with enough money to help those who might have followed our path, but I brought murder with me. I saved Jim at Eaglehawk Neck only to kill him in Backwater Woods under the tree where we played.'

Now, at last, he brushed away a tear. 'There's my story, gentlemen. I hope it assists you.'

We also were quiet for a long while. Once again the panelled walls of Lord Backwater's library had heard a tale fully as strange as anything on their shelves.

Sherlock Holmes broke the silence. 'You should not reproach yourself, Mr Connors.'

'No, indeed,' said Lord Patrick. 'For forty years my father grieved in secret that his beloved foster-brother had gone to his death to protect him. If he was to die he would not have wanted better than to do so while protecting you.'

'You were right in one matter,' said Holmes, 'and wrong in another.'

'What were they?' asked Connors.

'You were right to believe that the Ring died when Norfolk Island closed,' he said.

'But surely, Holmes,' I protested, 'you identified the Ring's tattoos on Lord Backwater's arms, you heard his narrative, you've seen the letters. This must be the work of the Ring!'

'I do not say,' he said imperturbably, 'that this affair does not have its roots in the Ring, but I do say that the Ring is dead. It was an organisation that could only thrive on Norfolk Island, a thousand miles from anywhere, where both convicts and guards could be bent or threatened to its will. Its convict members are dead, sent to the Australian mainland or, in a very few cases, returned to England. Its soldier members too are either dead or scattered wherever the Army has sent them. In England the Ring has no closed and fearful community in which it can operate and only small numbers to do its bidding. The Ring has died.'

'Then, in what way was I wrong?' asked Connors.

'You were wrong,' replied Holmes, 'to believe that it is still the Ring that is hunting you.'

'Then who is it?' demanded Lord Backwater.

'There,' said my friend, uncoiling from his chair, 'lies the crux of the problem, to the solution of which I propose to devote some time. Perhaps, Lord Backwater, you will excuse me if I miss dinner. If you can have some coffee sent in to me here I shall consider what we now know in greater detail.'

At dinner we racked our brains to see what Holmes had meant, but with no success. After the meal Arnold was about to take more coffee to Holmes but I relieved him of the duty.

The library was thick with tobacco smoke and Holmes sat, leaning back from the table, gazing through narrowed eyes at a row of items laid out in front of him. I saw that they were Inspector Scott's photographs and my own sketch of the marks on Williams' violin.

'You have not made sense of the marks, then?' I enquired as I poured his coffee.

'No,' he said. 'Why, Watson, why would he begin with a letter and then make only spots?'

'I cannot imagine,' I said, 'but are you sure the four spots are meaningful?'

'There are, in fact, five spots,' he said.

'But I drew only four,' I said.

'So you did. But if you look at the photograph you will see a fifth mark, to the right and on a level with the second one.'

I picked up the picture. 'There is a mark there,' I conceded, 'but I took it for a mere smear.'

'I grant you that it is less pronounced,' said Holmes, 'but I believe it is intentional.'

'But if he wrote the "J", surely these marks are only where his fingers fell as his strength gave out?'

'They cannot be,' said Holmes and passed me his lens 'Take a look through that.'

I examined each spot carefully but failed to see any difference. 'They all look alike to me,' I confessed.

'Precisely,' said Holmes, 'so they cannot be the marks of different fingers. The lens reveals that each spot includes an impression of the same scar, even the fifth. They are the deliberate marks of one finger applied five times.'

'Perhaps it is not a "J",' I suggested. 'Might it not be a "G" or an "I"?'

'It is not, I think, a "G",' said Holmes. 'The loop is all wrong. I suppose that it might be interpreted as an "I", but either would leave the same fundamental problem. What is the significance of a single letter followed by a row of blobs?'

He looked at the photograph again as I gave it back. 'Curse the man!' he said. 'I offered him safety from the rope if he would tell us what he knew and he showed us the door with a torrent of abuse. Then he leaves this singularly obscure message.'

'Maybe he threw us out because you played and sang to him,' I joked.

'So I did,' he mused. 'I played his strange instrument and I sang him — Watson, that's it!' he exclaimed.

I stared at him dumbstruck. 'Don't you see?' he demanded. 'Williams knew that I was a musician. If he left a message accessible to the first comer it might have been destroyed, so he left a message that only a musician would see.'

Before I could make any reply he snatched the photograph from the table and dashed out of the room. I followed him into the drawing-room, where Lord Backwater and Connors were conversing over a decanter. With no apology Holmes rushed to the piano and flung up the lid.

'Listen!' he commanded. 'Does this remind any of you of anything?' and he picked out a short phrase with one finger.

He turned and we shook our heads. He repeated the phrase a number of times, each time changing the pitch. Still none of us saw any resemblance to anything we recalled.

Holmes looked at our puzzled faces. 'I have evidently not solved all the puzzle,' he remarked, and left the room as swiftly as he had entered.

'Does this have something to do with the case?' asked Lord Patrick.

'I am sure it does,' I said, 'though precisely what I do not know. I can only say that this mood usually presages some astounding insight into a problem.'

I rejoined Holmes in the library. He had fallen back into his previous position, scanning the photograph.

'I must be right,' he said. 'It must be music.'

'I do not follow you,' I admitted.

'You yourself asked, Watson, why the initial "J" followed by mere spots. That is because it is not a "J". It is the treble clef, hence the spots that follow it are notes.'

'I see,' I said, 'but they do not seem to make any recognisable tune. Surely he would have used something obvious?'

'Indeed he would,' said Holmes. 'So I have still missed something here.'

'Maybe they are letters,' I hazarded. 'You have shown me that some codes consist of symbols replacing letters. Musical notes are named by letters.'

He stared at me. 'Watson!' he exclaimed. 'I never understand you. Sometimes you do not grasp the obvious but occasionally you produce sparks of sheer brilliance.'

He snatched a sheet of paper and scribbled. 'It cannot be FDGGD,' he muttered. 'Oh, Watson, Watson... what might you have become if only you had systematised your thought processes?'

I did not know whether to be pleased by his praise or offended by his last comment, but suddenly he straightened up.

His eyes gleamed as he looked at his note. 'Yes, Watson, brilliant,' he repeated. 'Now, I think I have all that I need to complete my enquiries. Please ask Lord Backwater to send a message to the Superintendent to meet me here at ten tomorrow morning,' and with a curt 'good night' he dismissed me.

Twenty-Three

A FINAL REPORT

Holmes was early at breakfast and with a keen appetite. He deflected all questions about the case, remarking only that he fully expected to have concluded the entire affair by noon.

When Superintendent Thorpe arrived, accompanied by the young constable, Holmes would only tell him that he was now in possession of all the facts, that he proposed to present a final report to the Chief Constable and that, in view of the Colonel's hostility to him, he wished the Superintendent to be present.

At the Chief Constable's door we were met by his manservant in shirt-sleeves. He apologised, explaining that the Colonel was enjoying his daily sword and pistol exercises and for that reason we would not be able to see him.

'I feel sure he would wish to see me,' said Holmes, and strode past the protesting servant into the hall. We followed and the Colonel's man could do nothing except dart nervously ahead of us, repeating his objections.

We followed him to a large room at the rear of the house. It was evidently once the ballroom but had been converted into an exercise area.

The walls were racked with firearms and swords. Near us was a table on which lay pistols and ammunition and beyond it stood a mechanical exercise horse. At the far end of the room stairs led up to a gallery, once intended for musicians. The area beneath the gallery had targets displayed on the walls, which showed more bullet-pocks than our sitting-room wall in Baker Street.

Colonel Caddage stood by the mechanical horse, in a loose, old-fashioned shirt, trousers and top-boots. A sabre dangled from his right hand. It struck me that, despite his years, he looked like some blood of the Regency era.

'What the devil?' he snarled as we entered. 'Oh, it's you, Holmes. I should have expected even you to have the manners to go away when you're not welcome. As for you, Thorpe, it'll cost you your place if there's no good reason for this intrusion.'

'I have come,' said Holmes, 'to present my final conclusions in the case of Lord Backwater.'

'And what are they?' sneered the Chief Constable. 'Now that Williams and the other two are dead, have you come to tell me that it was poachers all along?'

'It was not,' said Holmes evenly, 'poachers who killed Inspector Scott.'

'Then tell us your conclusions, by all means,' said the Colonel.

'Firstly,' began Holmes, 'I have been examining your own career.'

The Colonel's eyes flickered. 'You impertinent scoundrel!' he grated. 'What has that got to do with anything?'

'Only this,' said my friend, 'that you come of an undistinguished country family so that, when you chose the Army as a career, you were commissioned in a less fashionable regiment, having to accept postings that lacked fashionable interest.'

'I shall not,' warned the Colonel, 'stand to be insulted in my own home for very long.'

'I shall not be very long,' said Holmes. 'The facts are simple. As a young officer you were posted to Norfolk Island and there you murdered a brother officer, one Lieutenant Dawson.'

'Damn you!' roared the Colonel. 'You muck-raking jackanapes! Dawson took his own life. If you do not withdraw that lie, I–'

Holmes ignored the outburst and pressed on, 'Dawson died by your hand, Colonel. There were no powder burns on his waistcoat and, before you replaced it, the pistol was across the table.'

Caddage's eyes stood out like organ stops. 'You have questioned...' he began, then stopped.

'You were,' said Holmes, 'about to say that I have been questioning the former convict Connors, with whose help you succeeded in making Dawson's death look like suicide. In return, and so that Connors could not blackmail you, you connived at – nay – arranged his escape from Norfolk Island.'

A storm of emotions was raging across the Colonel's face. Holmes continued. 'In the wake of the Chinese War you were sent to Hong Kong and there, by a fluke of chance, you saw Connors again, though that was not the name he used. You have always been a greedy man, Colonel. Even at Norfolk Island you found ways to accumulate wealth. Connors had a valuable pearl to sell and, when you found that out, you tried to blackmail him for a portion of the proceeds. When he fled, you had him hounded.

'The whole of the British possessions in the East and around the Pacific were full of two kinds of Britons, soldiers and ex-convicts. It was easy for you to use the Ring to keep track of him and to threaten him.'

'The Ring!' snorted Colonel Caddage. 'An invention of cheap novelists and do-gooders!'

'Was it, indeed?' said Holmes. 'Perhaps you will be so kind as to turn back your sleeves and prove to us that you were not a Brother of the Ring.

No? I thought that you would not. No matter. There came a day when you were posted back to England and lost track of Connors, but you had sufficient wealth from one source and another to purchase this splendid estate in your native county. Here, in retirement, you achieved apparent honour and respect.

'There the story would have ended, but for the unlucky fact that this county is also Connors' home and, when you had ceased to hunt him, he began to visit Backwater. Your faithful henchman and Brother of the Ring, Williams, will have reported the comings and goings from the Backwater Arms of an outspoken radical from London, and your investigations revealed your old quarry. You could not believe your good fortune. His movements were watched and, a few days ago, Williams led two more Brothers to the ambush in the beech glade that resulted in Lord Backwater's death.'

The Colonel's face had settled to a mask of white, out of which his eyes burned black. 'You have no proof,' he said.

'It might be found,' said Holmes airily. 'It had already dawned on you that Connors, being illegally returned to England and living under a false name, had left his money in the care of Lord Backwater. When Connors escaped your net you had Lady Patricia Backwater abducted and sought to extract money from her brother.

'There are some things, it seems, at which even the villainous Williams rebelled,' he went on. 'He sought to speak to me and Inspector Scott heard the message given to Dr Watson. The Inspector reported that to you in his nightly report and by the time he and Watson called on Williams the next day he was dead at the hands of your minions.'

'By God, Holmes,' growled the Colonel, 'your lying effrontery has no limits. You shall pay for this!'

Holmes ignored the threat. 'As Inspector Scott left here on the eve of his death he spoke to Superintendent Thorpe. He said that he must ask

Dr Watson something that would confirm his suspicions of someone. Mr Thorpe innocently repeated that remark to you and you knew that Scott must be stopped before he exposed you.'

'Why do you say so, Mr Holmes?' said Thorpe, who had stood like a statue throughout Holmes' revelations.

'Scott intended to ask Watson if anyone else had heard of Williams' message. If Watson had told no one, then the only other person who had known was Colonel Caddage and it must have been the Colonel who had Williams killed. So, his henchmen dead, the Colonel must shift to ambush Scott himself and shoot him down.'

'This is all very interesting,' broke in the Colonel, 'but so far you have advanced only theories, presumably because you have no single item of proof.'

'I do beg your pardon, Colonel,' said Holmes. 'Have I forgotten to tell you that I have absolute proof of what Williams wished to tell me?' and he reached in his coat pocket, withdrawing one of the photographs.

'Here,' he said, 'is a photograph of the very clear message that Williams left me, in which he identifies you as the progenitor of the crimes in which he was involved,' and he held it out to Colonel Caddage.

Caddage snatched it with his left hand and stared at it. 'This is that stupid tin violin of Williams!' he snorted. 'And someone has scribbled on it. Since, Holmes, you have evidently been prying into the Army List to learn my history, you might have taken the trouble to observe that my forenames are Gerald Oliver. What is written here is plainly a "J" and has no relation to me.'

He thrust the card back at Holmes who ignored it. He was smiling thinly, for he enjoyed nothing so much as the successful denouement of his theories. I, however, was watching the Colonel's white, hard face, and remembering that he still held a sabre in his right hand.

'It is not,' said my friend, 'a "J". It is the treble clef. Are you musical, Colonel? I think not as your ballroom serves as a firing range and gymnasium. Nevertheless, you may take my word for it that what follows that symbol is a row of notes and that those notes spell out—'

'More of your incompetent nonsense,' sneered Caddage. 'There are no stave lines. Even if these are intended for notes you cannot determine which notes are intended.'

'So you are musical, after all,' said Holmes pleasantly. 'Then you will agree with me that we ordinarily use only seven notes, each identified by a letter. Thus there are only seven possibilities in that line of dots. They might, I grant you, be DBEEB, but that would be meaningless. As would ECFFC, or FDGGD, or GEAAE, AFBBF or BGCCG. In fact, only one sequence makes any kind of sense – CADDA – which, apart from forming the first five letters of your name, is, so far as I know, the beginning of no other word or name in the English language. There is no doubt, Colonel, that Williams named you.'

The sword swung in the air and Caddage slashed at Holmes, screaming, 'Damn you! Damn you! Damn you! I'll not hang for a crawling convict and a prying Cockney muck-raker!'

Holmes slipped under the sabre's arc with a fluidity surprising in so tall a man. In a moment he had possessed himself of a weapon from the wall-racks.

'If we are to try conclusions in this fashion,' he began, 'I should warn you—' but Caddage cut him short.

'Do tell me,' he sneered, and a mad light of battle was in his eyes, 'that you did a little fencing at college and you fancy yourself my match!'

'I was about to remark,' said Holmes, 'that at the age of fourteen years I enrolled with Maître Alphonse Bencin, considered to be the finest swordsman in Europe. After four years of his tuition he thought well of my abilities.'

He lunged suddenly at the Colonel, and with a flurry of well-directed blows drove him back to the foot of the stairs leading to the gallery. There Caddage was able to hold him at bay for a while, but the relentless strength of Holmes' strokes drove the Colonel, step by step, up the stairway.

At the head of the stairs, and before Holmes had reached the gallery, Caddage swung suddenly as though to run down the landing, then turned instantly back and drove a murderous blow at my friend's midriff. Holmes' sabre smashed the Colonel's blade upwards, so that the hilts of their weapons locked above their heads and they reeled and twisted along the gallery in a grotesque waltz.

They had reached the far end of the little gallery when their twisting flung them against the balustrade. With a snap like a pistol-shot the old woodwork gave way under their combined weight and in a whirl of arms and legs they fell to the floor of the exercise room.

Both were on their feet in a flash, but Holmes had lost his weapon in the fall. As he stooped to grasp it the Colonel was on him, driving his sabre point at my friend's unprotected chest.

I groped in my pocket for my pistol but I knew there was no time to aim and fire. My hand had just closed around the butt when a shot rang from behind me and Caddage stopped dead. The sabre point dropped and he staggered back, a look of astonishment crossing his face. Then the sword clattered to the floor and he fell backwards beside it.

Twenty-Four

SUPERINTENDENT THORPE'S CONCLUSIONS

I turned to see Patrick Connors standing by the table, a smoking pistol in his hand. As I watched he handed it to Superintendent Thorpe.

I looked to see if Holmes required assistance, but he was brushing his coat and referred me to the Colonel.

Caddage lay on his back, his right hand clutching his shirt where an extremely accurate shot had taken him in the heart. He still breathed and waved me away, not wishing, I imagine, to be saved for the noose, but it was evident to me that he would not survive long. Nor did he; in minutes he was gone.

Patrick Connors sat at the gun table, coolly smoking a cheroot, and Superintendent Thorpe sat opposite, making a note in his pocket-book. It occurred to me that Connors, by saving Holmes, had placed himself in grave danger.

As Holmes and I walked over the Superintendent looked up from his pocket-book.

'I have,' he said, 'been jotting down the particulars of this event while they are still fresh in my memory. If you will be so good, gentlemen, I should like to read what I have written and, if you agree with my account of events, I shall ask each of you to sign it, making it the official contemporary record of what has passed here this morning.'

We nodded and he cleared his throat and read us what he had written:

"'At ten o'clock in the forenoon, together with PC 112 Wetherby, I attended Mr Sherlock Holmes, consulting detective of 221B Baker Street, London and his associate, Dr Watson. Mr Holmes had sent a message that he wished me to meet him at Backwater Hall. On my arrival he informed me that he wished me to accompany him to the home of Colonel Caddage, Chief Constable of the county. I knew that Mr Holmes had been retained by Lord Backwater to investigate the former Lord Backwater's death and events which appeared to arise therefrom. I understood that he wished me to be present when he put certain facts and conclusions to Colonel Caddage, perhaps so that I could make an arrest.

"'We proceeded to Colonel Caddage's home where we were taken to the Colonel's exercise room by his manservant. The Colonel had been exercising himself with pistols and at sword-play. Mr Holmes then put to the Colonel the following propositions:

"'One, that while a serving officer of the garrison at Norfolk Island the Colonel had murdered a brother officer, one Lieutenant Dawson, and arranged and connived at the escape of a convict youth called Connors.

"'Two, that, coming to learn of Connors' return to England and that he had visited the Backwater vicinity, Colonel Caddage, being fearful of exposure, conspired with Elihu Williams and two others (all now deceased) to lie in wait for Connors and injure or kill him.

"'Three, that the late Lord Backwater fell by accident into the ambush set for Connors and was killed.

"'Four, that the Colonel then conspired with the same associates who had murdered Lord Backwater to abduct and unlawfully imprison Lady

Patricia Backwater and two of her servants, by which means he extorted the sum of fifty thousand pounds sterling from Lord Backwater.

"'Five, that, learning of an intention of Elihu Williams to inform on his plots, the Colonel conspired with the same two confederates to compass the death of Williams.

"'And six, that on being informed by the writer that Inspector Scott believed he knew who was responsible for these crimes, the Colonel lay in wait for Inspector Scott and shot him dead.

"'Colonel Caddage denied all knowledge of these matters. Mr Holmes then informed him that he was in possession of proof that Elihu Williams had, in his dying moments, left clear evidence that he knew Colonel Caddage to be the originator of the crimes in which Williams had been involved. This proof he explained to the Colonel, establishing it by producing a photograph taken at the scene of Williams' death on the order of Inspector Scott.

"'Colonel Caddage then abused Mr Holmes and attacked him with a sabre. Mr Holmes defended himself and a fight ensued in which no one else present had any opportunity to intervene. Eventually Mr Holmes found himself at the Colonel's mercy and it was evident that Colonel Caddage intended to kill Mr Holmes before all of us. Fortunately, we were joined at that point by Mr Peter Collins, a guest of Lord Backwater, who had come in search of Mr Holmes. With commendable promptness he snatched up one of the Colonel's practice pistols and shot at Colonel Caddage, thereby, in my submission, saving Mr Holmes' life. Dr Watson gave medical assistance to Colonel Caddage, but he expired shortly afterwards.'"

He stopped and walked over to where Colonel Caddage lay. Stooping, he turned back the Colonel's cuffs. He straightened up, jotted something in his pocket-book and rejoined us.

'Pardon me, gentlemen,' he said. 'Where was I? Ah, yes – "Upon the Colonel's death I examined his body and saw for myself that he bore old tattooing in the form of patterns which I understand to be characteristic of those worn by members of a former secret society at Norfolk Island. These indicated to me that he had sworn a treasonable oath under the Mutiny Act of 1797 and had, most probably, engaged in common law offences of conspiracy.

'"The events herein described took place in my presence and hearing and that of my constable, the Colonel's manservant and Dr Watson. I have asked all present to sign this record to certify that it meets their recollection of events. In a more detailed report I shall explain Mr Holmes' proof of Williams' information. I recommend that no action should be taken against any surviving participant."'

He looked at our silent faces. 'I regret,' he said, 'that I have had to simplify your very clever deductions in this matter, Mr Holmes, but it seemed to me that my report should not be over-complicated by unnecessary detail.'

'Oh, entirely, Superintendent,' said Holmes. 'If that is your professional assessment of the situation I am sure that none of us here would disagree.'

'That,' said the Superintendent, 'is my considered opinion. I told you, I believe, that Inspector Scott was a personal friend of mine. I thank you both – you, Mr Holmes, and you, Mr Collins – that you have brought his murderer to justice and that I was present to see it. Now, if there is nothing further, gentlemen, I shall be grateful if you will sign this record and then I must be about clearing this matter up and informing my superiors.'

As we rode away Holmes thanked Connors. 'That was,' he said, 'a very pretty piece of shooting, but you put yourself at a fearful risk. How did you come to be there?'

'In conversation with Lord Backwater he mentioned where you had gone. I recognised the name, of course, and was determined to see you challenge him. When the moment arose it was no trouble to take one of his own pistols and down him. If Superintendent Thorpe had been less reasonable I should not have objected. I had done my duty by Jim.'

'But why did Scott wish to consult me?' I enquired.

'Watson,' sighed Holmes, 'as I explained to the late Colonel Caddage, Scott had realised, as I should have done much earlier, that it was most probably when he reported to Caddage that Williams intended to talk that Caddage decided to murder his former associate. He merely wished to confirm that you, he, Arnold and Caddage were the only persons who knew.'

'I see,' I said, 'and all my "brilliance" about the music was wasted.'

'There you are wrong, Watson,' said my friend. 'I admit that I broke my own rules and assumed that the corrupt Lieutenant at Norfolk Island had nothing to do with recent events. When collecting data one should take account of all available information, without making previous decisions as to relevance. Then it occurred to me that a connection between Norfolk Island, Hong Kong and England might be a soldier, but by then you had drawn my attention to the correct solution of Williams' clue. A little research in the Army Lists confirmed Williams' information, and Williams' clue I could use to threaten Caddage without invoking the testimony of an escaped convict illegally returned to England.'

As we made our way home by train on the next day, Holmes remarked, 'A singular case, Watson, that led from rural England to the Old Hell in the Pacific.'

'Well,' I said, 'at least the System is over now.'

'Yes,' he said, 'but the harm that it did will continue to work. Now the Australians are busy putting the shadow of the System behind them,

Van Diemen's Land has a new name, but it will come back to haunt them and us. One day Australia will rise to nationhood and, when she does, is it not possible that she will remember the cruelties of her childhood and seek to turn against her parent? I should not be surprised. The Americans fought a war with us for far less.'

A last footnote to the Backwater case caught my eye in the following morning's paper, which recorded that Chief Constable Caddage had died as the result of an accident with a pistol in his gun-room. I passed it to Holmes. 'Someone,' he said, 'wishes to be discreet, but then, you and I are never anything else.'

So it is that in thirty years I have mentioned, but never before detailed, the service that Sherlock Holmes did for Lord Backwater.

Author's Notes

As with the previous manuscripts which I have edited for publication *(Sherlock Holmes and the Railway Maniac, Sherlock Holmes and the Devil's Grail)*, I have made such checks as I can on the authenticity of the document. No one possesses an indisputable sample of John Watson's handwriting, though the writing of the manuscript matches the most likely specimens. His habit of blending real and imaginary names (and, quite possibly, altering dates) does not help. Where I have been able to check statements of fact, they make sense, and there is, towards the end, one item which strongly suggests that the document is indeed of Watson's creation.

It is only right that I should record my gratitude here to Robert Hughes. His fact-filled, pithy, perceptive and witty history of the System, *The Fatal Shore* (Collins Harvill, 1987; Pan Books, 1988), has been of enormous value to me in checking out details of transportation.

CHAPTER ONE

The initial problem is almost always the same – who was the client and where was the action? In two published references to this case Watson tells us only that, at a later date, Lord Backwater trained racehorses in Hampshire. Now there is (and was) no such title, and no such place as Backwater, in Hampshire or anywhere else in England. That this story does not take place in Hampshire is proved by the arrival from Paddington and the fact that Backwater lay beyond Swindon. If I were forced to guess I would suggest Gloucestershire or Somerset.

CHAPTER THREE

That Holmes knew so much about tattoos will be no surprise to those who have read Baring Gould's *A Biography of Mr Sherlock Holmes: The World's First Consulting Detective* (Hart-Davis, 1962; Panther, 1975), where it is recorded that Holmes had privately published his monograph 'Upon Tattoo Marks' in 1878 and that it included "one of the first scholarly examinations of the pigments used extensively by Japanese and Chinese artists."

The "fox chase" to which Watson refers was the ultimate glory of the seaport tattooist's art – a fox hunt in full cry and full colour, men, horses and hounds, sweeping down from the shoulders across the back, in pursuit of a fox whose brush could be seen disappearing into the only available earth. I believe that the last wearer of it discovered in England was, in fact, an Admiral, throwing, maybe, further doubt on Lombroso's opinion that tattoos are a mark of criminality.

The 'EVER' and 'NEVER' tattoos are still to be seen among older convicts, though they probably adopted them from old crime novels without a real knowledge of their significance. The 'gang mark' under the pad of the left thumb seemed to be a Scottish practice and was still to be seen in the 1960s.

CHAPTER FIVE

The first novel written by a transported convict was *Ralph Rashleigh* by Giacomo de Rosenberg, almost certainly the penname of James Rogers, a convict clerk transported for blackmail. Although fiction, the book is closely based on episodes in the lives of the writer and other convicts.

Rogers was, for a while, playwright and producer for a convict drama group, and describes how the lack of suitable woods and skills drove them to construct musical instruments from tin. John Bunyan (before the Lord told him that the violin was an instrument of the Devil) was both a blacksmith and a fiddler. Lacking the wherewithal to buy an instrument, he produced one in wrought iron which, I believe, still survives.

More remarkable than Williams' instrument is Holmes' ability to play it straight away, for it was 'back-strung', that is strung for a left-handed player. Any right-handed player will recognise how extremely skilful Holmes' feat was.

The sad, slow melody was an Irish rebel song from the 1798 Rebellion, known as 'Boolavogue' or 'Father Murphy's Air'. In Australia it attached itself to a song called 'Moreton Bay' or 'The Convicts' Lament on the Death of Captian Logan'. Logan was the sadistic Commandant of the Moreton Bay Station (where Brisbane now stands) and was killed by aborigines while out hunting in 1830. Forty-nine years later, when the bushranger Ned Kelly addressed his 'Jerilderie Letter' to the people of Australia, he paraphrased the song:

Port McQuarrie Toweringabbie Norfolk Island and Emu Plains
and in those places of tyranny and condemnation
many a blooming Irish man rather than subdue to the Saxon yoke
were flogged to death and bravely died in servile chains.

CHAPTER EIGHT

The peepshow was an extremely popular forerunner of the mobile cinema and appeared at British fairs for many years. It was usually a long box with viewing apertures along its sides. Inside, the operator constructed with coloured papers, scenes of popular drama, celebrated crimes, etc., lit by lamps. A penny (or in poor districts, a pin) enabled one to stand at a viewing window and be amazed by the splendour of the scene. The father of Lord George Sanger, the circus manager, operated a peepshow for many years.

CHAPTER NINE

The anti-machine riots that swept the South-West in 1831 caused a panic-stricken government to appoint a Special Commission of Judges to sit at Winchester. Although no one had been harmed by the rioters (the only death was of a bystander, shot by a nervous soldier), the Commission issued five hundred transportation and one hundred death sentences, most of which were later commuted to transportation. Among those actually hanged was a nineteen-year-old called Cook, who had broken the hat of Mr Baring, the banker. Hampshire legend says that the snow never lies on Cook's grave.

With the American War of Independence, the practice of shipping convicts to America had to end. For a few years, as the expanding industrial cities swelled the crime rate, the prisons filled up and overflowed into the 'hulks' – dismasted ships moored at almost every port and used as additional prisons. Once transportation to Australia began the hulks continued in use as assembly prisons.

CHAPTER TEN

The route to Van Diemen's Land described is the usual one – down the Atlantic to Rio, then across to pass round the Cape of Good Hope and east to Australia. With no Suez or Panama Canals it was the best way to take advantage of prevailing winds, even so it was a sixteen-thousand mile voyage and took months. The First Fleet in 1788 called at Cape Town as well.

The term "hoof" appears in Partridge's *Dictionary of the Underworld*, supported by testimony from an Old Bailey trial in 1833 to explain its meaning as "a person of unnatural propensities". Partridge does not give it the dignity of being the first recorded instance of rhyming slang (that honour he gives to "lord of the manor = tanner" a few years later), but the modern English rhyming slang is 'iron = iron hoof = poof' and the Australian is 'horse's hoof'. The term "night cocky" is definitely rhyming slang, 'cocky = cockatoo = screw', and must have developed in the System, though it is still in use in Britain. The more modern equivalent is 'kanga = kangaroo = screw', brought to us by the Convicts' Revenge – Aussie soap operas.

An illustration of the fearsome security fence at Eagle-hawk Neck appears in Robert Hughes, *The Fatal Shore*.

The ritual of the Ring is different from that described by Marcus Clarke in *His Natural Life* though the chant is the same. Clarke interviewed survivors of Norfolk Island about the Ring, but they were very unwilling to talk about it. Nowhere else have I seen it suggested that the Ring operated outside Norfolk Island, but it cannot be proved that it did not.

CHAPTER TWELVE

The reference to Port Arthur sending messages to Hobart in an hour must mean the semaphore-type signalling system that was established at Port Arthur with 'repeater stations' all the way to Hobart, so that escaping convicts would be outrun by the news. Similar systems had been in use in Britain for many years, particularly to carry urgent news from the Channel ports to London. Many Telegraph Hills in England owe their names to these devices.

Pearce the man-eater was a real character. Transported from Ireland for stealing shoes, he was first assigned as a servant, but kept absconding, stealing and boozing. When flogging failed he was sent to Macquarie Harbour. There, in September 1822, he was one of eight convicts who stole a boat and escaped. They intended to cross Van Diemen's Land to the River Derwent, steal a schooner and sail home out of Hobart. As they floundered through the forested mountains the weather turned to sleet and their rations ran out. One of their number was killed for food, prompting two to turn back. Kennelly and Brown, the two dropouts, were recaptured but died within days. After twenty-five days the escapers reached the plains and there another man was killed for food. Eventually only Pearce and a man called Greenhill were left, Greenhill carrying the only weapon, an axe. For two days and nights they watched each other like hawks, until Pearce succeeded in killing Greenhill. Shortly after, he reached the Derwent and, after a variety of adventures, became one of a team of bush-rangers. They were all captured in January 1823, but when Pearce dictated his grim story to a clergyman nobody believed it – they thought he was covering for friends still on the run and simply shipped him back to Macquarie Harbour. He certainly didn't tell his story there, because in October he bolted again, in company with a man called Owen. Within days Owen was dead and partly eaten and Pearce was captured. This time the evidence of Owen's remains convinced the authorities. Pearce was hanged and his body handed over to anatomists. His skull was preserved and is still on display in the American Academy of Natural Sciences. Pearce was the best-known but not the only convict bolter who took to cannibalism.

From Lord Backwater's description of the striped beast, it sounds as if he encountered the rarest of Tasmania's native animals, the Tasmanian Tiger. Although one has never been captured, filmed or photographed, it has been sighted often enough for zoologists to accept that it not only did, but does exist.

As far as I know, no boys from Point Puer are recorded as having escaped across the Neck, and the circumstances of Lord Backwater and his foster-brother mean that they would not have been so recorded. Nevertheless, when Marcus Clarke embarked upon his epic novel of the System, *His Natural Life*, in the 1870s, he included an episode involving two orphans attempting to escape from Point Puer. Unable to escape and unwilling to return, they decide on suicide and what follows is the finest of all Victorian tear-jerking scenes:

'Will it hurt much, Tommy?' said Billy, who was not so courageous.

'Not so much as a whipping.'

'I'm afraid! Oh, Tom, it's so deep! Don't leave me, Tom!'

The bigger baby took his little handkerchief from his neck, and with it bound his left hand to his companion's right.

'Now I can't leave you.'

'What was it the Lady that kissed us said, Tommy?'

'Lord have pity on them two fatherless children!' repeated Tommy.

'Let's say it, Tom.'

And so the two babies knelt down on the brink of the cliff, and raising the bound hands together, looked up at the sky, and said, 'Lord have pity on us two fatherless children!' And then they kissed each other and did it.

Robert Hughes records that the publication of Clarke's book brought tourists to Port Arthur, most of whom wanted to see the spot where this fictitious event occurred, but one has to wonder if Clarke, whose researches were formidable, had not come across a version of Lord Backwater's story and amended it for his audience.

CHAPTER THIRTEEN

All of the security precautions mentioned were in force at Hobart. Every departing vessel was searched by police and soldiers and sulphur-candles burned below decks to smoke out stowaways. If an escaper was found on board, the master and every member of the crew were fined a month's pay. Conversely, if an informer caused the capture of an escapee he was rewarded with a month's pay and given the right to take his discharge from the vessel.

Yerba Bueno, where Lord Backwater landed in California, shortly became better known as San Francisco.

The Fenian escape to which he refers occurred only ten years before the date of the present narrative. The last convict transport, the *Hugoumont*, sailed from Portland in 1868, carrying, among others, sixty Irish rebels convicted in the previous year's Fenian revolt. It was the boast of the Fenian Brotherhood that, whatever the English did to captured Fenians, the Brotherhood would come to their aid. For years they planned to strike a blow against the System. Using couriers between Ireland, England, America and Australia, the Brotherhood arranged the purchase of a whaling-ship, the *Catalpa*, in New England and sailed her into Australian waters on what seemed to be a genuine whaling trip. Her captain had orders to lie off Fremantle until six prisoners could escape from a road gang. Just as the American ship picked up the convicts, a British steamer, the *Georgette*, appeared, loaded with Marines, and fired a shot across *Catalpa's* bows. Caught in British waters by a faster vessel *Catalpa's* master hoisted the Stars and Stripes and tried to bluff his way out, but the *Georgette* came on. Then, when it seemed that capture was inevitable, *Georgette* fell back. She had been coaling in Fremantle when news of the escape reached her and had set out without completing. After burning her wooden fittings she finally ran out of steam and had to let *Catalpa* go.

CHAPTER EIGHTEEN

Until mechanised refrigeration became widespread there were only two ways of chilling food and drink. One was the ice-making machine, a device which required cranking by hand for a long time. The other was the ice-house. These were brick-lined, underground chambers into which ice was stacked in winter in such quantities that, hopefully, it would last through the summer. As well as cutting ice on local water in cold winters, suppliers brought shiploads to Britain from Europe, Scandinavia and even from the lakes of North America.

CHAPTER TWENTY-ONE

It is the case that convicts at Norfolk Island became so desperate that they drew lots in the kind of 'suicide club' described by Connors. Eventually the authorities began sitting courts on the island, believing that it was the trip to Sydney and the chance of escape that fired the practice, but it did not die out because, for some, it was the certainty of death that appealed to them.

CHAPTER TWENTY-THREE

Difficult as it is to confirm the authenticity of this narrative, a pointer may be found in Holmes' statement that he had been a pupil of Maître Bencin. W. S. Baring-Gould, in the biography already cited above, asserts that Holmes' family spent two periods living at Pau in the

South of France. The second period began, he says, in 1868, when Sherlock was fourteen, and it was then that his father enrolled him with Maître Alphonse Bencin. Unfortunately, Baring-Gould never revealed the source of his information.

The above notes reflect my researches so far but do not, I am afraid, absolutely confirm Watson's authorship of the narrative. However, I would point out that this story originates from the same source as the two others which I have edited, both of which contained better confirmations of their authenticity. I would argue that if they were the work of Dr Watson, so is the present account.

Barrie Roberts
1996

Also Available

the further adventures of

SHERLOCK HOLMES

THE VEILED DETECTIVE

by

DAVID STUART DAVIES

AFGHANISTAN,
THE EVENING OF 27 JUNE 1880

The full moon hovered like a spectral observer over the British camp. The faint cries of the dying and wounded were carried by the warm night breeze out into the arid wastes beyond. John Walker staggered out of the hospital tent, his face begrimed with dried blood and sweat. For a moment he threw his head back and stared at the wide expanse of starless sky as if seeking an answer, an explanation. He had just lost another of his comrades. There were now at least six wounded men whom he had failed to save. He was losing count. And, by God, what was the point of counting in such small numbers anyway? Hundreds of British soldiers had died that day, slaughtered by the Afghan warriors. They had been outnumbered, outflanked and routed by the forces of Ayub Khan in that fatal battle at Maiwand. These cunning tribesmen had truly rubbed the Union Jack into the desert dust. Nearly a third of the company had fallen. It was only the reluctance of the Afghans to carry out further carnage that had prevented the British troops from being completely annihilated. Ayub Khan had his victory. He had made his point. Let the survivors report the news of his invincibility.

For the British, a ragged retreat was the only option. They withdrew into the desert, to lick their wounds and then to limp back to Candahar. They had had to leave their dead littering the bloody scrubland, soon to be prey to the vultures and vermin.

Walker was too tired, too sick to his stomach to feel anger, pain or frustration. All he knew was that when he trained to be a doctor, it had been for the purpose of saving lives. It was not to watch young men's pale, bloody faces grimace with pain and their eyes close gradually as life ebbed away from them, while he stood by, helpless, gazing at a gaping wound spilling out intestines.

He needed a drink. Ducking back into the tent, he grabbed his medical bag. There were still three wounded men lying on makeshift beds in there, but no amount of medical treatment could save them from the grim reaper. He felt guilty to be in their presence. He had instructed his orderly to administer large doses of laudanum to help numb the pain until the inevitable overtook them.

As Walker wandered to the edge of the tattered encampment, he encountered no other officer. Of course, there were very few left. Colonel MacDonald, who had been in charge, had been decapitated by an Afghan blade very early in the battle. Captain Alistair Thornton was now in charge of the ragged remnants of the company of the Berkshire regiment, and he was no doubt in his tent nursing his wound. He had been struck in the shoulder by a jezail bullet which had shattered the bone.

Just beyond the perimeter of the camp, Walker slumped down at the base of a skeletal tree, resting his back against the rough bark. Opening his medical bag, he extracted a bottle of brandy. Uncorking it, he sniffed the neck of the bottle, allowing the alcoholic fumes to drift up his nose. And then he hesitated.

Something deep within his conscience made him pause. Little did this tired army surgeon realise that he was facing a decisive moment of Fate. He was about to commit an act that would alter the course of his life for ever. With a frown, he shook the vague dark unformed thoughts from his mind and returned his attention to the bottle.

The tantalising fumes did their work. They promised comfort and oblivion. He lifted the neck of the bottle to his mouth and took a large gulp. Fire spilled down his throat and raced through his senses. Within moments he felt his body ease and relax, the inner tension melting with the warmth of the brandy. He took another gulp, and the effect increased. He had found an escape from the heat, the blood, the cries of pain and the scenes of slaughter. A blessed escape. He took another drink. Within twenty minutes the bottle was empty and John Walker was floating away on a pleasant, drunken dream. He was also floating away from the life he knew. He had cut himself adrift and was now heading for stormy, unchartered waters.

As consciousness slowly returned to him several hours later, he felt a sudden, sharp stabbing pain in his leg. It came again. And again. He forced his eyes open and bright sunlight seared in. Splinters of yellow light pierced his brain. He clamped his eyes shut, embracing the darkness once more. Again he felt the pain in his leg. This time, it was accompanied by a strident voice: "Walker! Wake up, damn you!"

He recognised the voice. It belonged to Captain Thornton. With some effort he opened his eyes again, but this time he did it more slowly, allowing the brightness to seep in gently so as not to blind him. He saw three figures standing before him, each silhouetted against the vivid blue sky of an Afghan dawn. One of them was kicking his leg viciously in an effort to rouse him.

"You despicable swine, Walker!" cried the middle figure, whose left arm was held in a blood-splattered sling. It was Thornton, his commanding officer.

Walker tried to get to his feet, but his body, still under the thrall of the alcohol, refused to co-operate.

"Get him up," said Thornton.

The two soldiers grabbed Walker and hauled him to his feet. With his good hand, Thornton thrust the empty brandy bottle before his face. For a moment, he thought the captain was going to hit him with it.

"Drunk on duty, Walker. No, by God, worse than that. Drunk while your fellow soldiers were in desperate need of your attention. You left them... left them to die while you... you went to get drunk. I should have you shot for this – but shooting is too good for you. I want you to live... to live with your guilt." Thornton spoke in tortured bursts, so great was his fury.

"There was nothing I could do for them," Walker tried to explain, but his words escaped in a thick and slurred manner. "Nothing I could–"

Thornton threw the bottle down into the sand. "You disgust me, Walker. You realise that this is a court martial offence, and believe me I shall make it my personal duty to see that you are disgraced and kicked out of the army."

Words failed Walker, but it began to sink in to his foggy mind that he had made a very big mistake – a life-changing mistake.

London, 4 October 1880

"Are you sure he can be trusted?" Arthur Sims sniffed and nodded towards the silhouetted figure at the end of the alleyway, standing under a flickering gas lamp.

Badger Johnson, so called because of the vivid white streak that ran through the centre of his dark thatch of hair, nodded and grinned.

"Yeah. He's a bit simple, but he'll be fine for what we want him for. And if he's any trouble…" He paused to retrieve a cut-throat razor from his inside pocket. The blade snapped open, and it swished through the air. "I'll just have to give him a bloody throat, won't I?"

Arthur Sims was not amused. "Where d'you find him?"

"Where d'you think? In The Black Swan. Don't you worry. I've seen him in there before – and I seen him do a bit of dipping. Very nifty he was, an' all. And he's done time. In Wandsworth. He's happy to be our crow for just five sovereigns."

"What did you tell him?"

"Hardly anything. What d'you take me for? Just said we were cracking a little crib in Hanson Lane and we needed a lookout. He's done the work before."

Sims sniffed again. "I'm not sure. You know as well as I do he ought to be vetted by the Man himself before we use him. If something goes wrong, we'll *all* have bloody throats… or worse."

Badger gurgled with merriment. "You scared, are you?"

"Cautious, that's all. This is a big job for us."

"And the pickin's will be very tasty, an' all, don't you worry. If it's cautious you're being, then you know it's in our best interest that we have a little crow keeping his beady eyes wide open. Never mind how much the Man has planned this little jaunt, *we're* the ones putting our heads in the noose."

Sims shuddered at the thought. "All right, you made your point. What's his name?"

"Jordan. Harry Jordan." Badger slipped his razor back into its special pocket and flipped out his watch. "Time to make our move."

Badger giggled as the key slipped neatly into the lock. "It's hardly criminal work if one can just walk in."

Arthur Sims gave his partner a shove. "Come on, get in," he whispered, and then he turned to the shadowy figure standing nearby. "OK, Jordan, you know the business."

Harry Jordan gave a mock salute.

Once inside the building, Badger lit the bull's-eye lantern and consulted the map. "The safe is in the office on the second floor at the far end, up a spiral staircase." He muttered the information, which he knew by heart anyway, as if to reassure himself now that theory had turned into practice.

The two men made their way through the silent premises, the thin yellow beam of the lamp carving a way through the darkness ahead of them. As the spidery metal of the staircase flashed into view, they spied an obstacle on the floor directly below it. The inert body of a bald-headed man.

Arthur Sims knelt by him. "Night watchman. Out like a light. Very special tea he's drunk tonight" Delicately, he lifted the man's eyelids to reveal the whites of his eyes. "He'll not bother us now, Badger. I reckon he'll wake up with a thundering headache around breakfast-time."

Badger giggled. It was all going according to plan.

Once up the staircase, the two men approached the room containing the safe. Again Badger produced the keyring from his pocket and slipped a key into the lock. The door swung open with ease. The bull's-eye soon located the imposing Smith-Anderson safe, a huge impenetrable iron contraption that stood defiantly in the far corner of the room. It was as tall as a man and weighed somewhere around three tons. The men knew from experience that the only way to get into this peter was by using the key – or rather the keys. There were five in all required. Certainly it would take a small army to move the giant safe, and God knows how much dynamite would be needed to blow it open, an act that would create enough noise to reach Scotland Yard itself.

Badger passed the bull's-eye to his confederate, who held the beam steady, centred on the great iron sarcophagus and the five locks. With another gurgle of pleasure, Badger dug deep into his trouser pocket and pulled out a brass ring containing five keys, all cut in a different manner. Scratched into the head of each key was a number – one that corresponded with the arrangement of locks on the safe.

Kneeling down in the centre of the beam, he slipped in the first key. It turned smoothly, with a decided click. So did the second. And the third. But the fourth refused to budge. Badger cast a worried glance at his confederate, but neither man spoke. Badger withdrew the key and tried again, with the same result. A thin sheen of sweat materialised on his brow. What the hell was wrong here? This certainly wasn't in the plan. The first three keys had been fine. He couldn't believe the Man had made a mistake. It was unheard of.

"Try the fifth key," whispered Arthur, who was equally perplexed and worried.

In the desperate need to take action of some kind, Badger obeyed. Remarkably, the fifth key slipped in easily and turned smoothly, with the same definite click as the first three. A flicker of hope rallied Badger's dampened spirits and he turned the handle of the safe. Nothing happened. It would not budge. He swore and sat back on his haunches. "What the hell now?"

"Try the fourth key again," came his partner's voice from the darkness.

Badger did as he was told and held his breath. The key fitted the aperture without problem. Now his hands were shaking and he paused, fearful of failure again.

"Come on, Badger."

He turned the key. At first there was some resistance, and then… it moved. It revolved. It clicked.

"The bastards," exclaimed Arthur Sims in a harsh whisper. "They've altered the arrangement of the locks so they can't be opened in order. His nibs ain't sussed that out."

Badger was now on his feet and tugging at the large safe door. "Blimey, it's a weight," he muttered, as the ponderous portal began to move. "It's bigger than my old woman," he observed, his spirits lightening again. The door creaked open with magisterial slowness. It took Badger almost a minute of effort before the safe door was wide open.

At last, Arthur Sims was able to direct the beam of the lantern to illuminate the interior of the safe. When he had done so, his jaw dropped and he let out a strangled gasp.

"What is it?" puffed Badger, sweat now streaming down his face.

"Take a look for yourself," came the reply.

As Badger pulled himself forward and peered round the corner of the massive safe door, a second lantern beam joined theirs. "The cupboard is bare, I am afraid."

The voice, clear, brittle and authoritative, came from behind them, and both felons turned in unison to gaze at the speaker.

The bull's-eye spotlit a tall young man standing in the doorway, a sardonic smile touching his thin lips. It was Harry Jordan. Or was it? He was certainly dressed in the shabby checked suit that Jordan wore – but where was the bulbous nose and large moustache?

"I am afraid the game is no longer afoot, gentlemen. I think the phrase is, 'You've been caught red-handed.' Now, please do not make any rash attempts to escape. The police are outside the building, awaiting my signal."

Arthur Sims and Badger Johnson stared in dumbfounded amazement as the young man took a silver whistle from his jacket pocket and blew on it three times. The shrill sound reverberated in their ears.

Inspector Giles Lestrade of Scotland Yard cradled a tin mug of hot, sweet tea in his hands and smiled contentedly. "I reckon that was a pretty good night's work."

It was an hour later, after the arrest of Badger Johnson and Arthur Sims, and the inspector was ensconced in his cramped office back at the Yard.

The young man sitting opposite him, wearing a disreputable checked suit which had seen better days, did not respond. His silence took the smile from Lestrade's face and replaced it with a furrowed brow.

"You don't agree, Mr Holmes?"

The young man pursed his lips for a moment before replying. "In a manner of speaking, it has been a successful venture. You have two of the niftiest felons under lock and key, and saved the firm of Meredith and Co. the loss of a considerable amount of cash."

"Exactly." The smile returned.

"But there are still questions left unanswered."

"Such as?"

"How did our two friends come into the possession of the key to the building, to the office where the safe was housed – and the five all-important keys to the safe itself?"

"Does that really matter?"

"Indeed it does. It is vital that these questions are answered in order to clear up this matter fully. There was obviously an accomplice involved who obtained the keys and was responsible for drugging the night-watchman. Badger Johnson intimated as much when he engaged my services as lookout, but when I pressed him for further information, he clammed up like a zealous oyster."

Lestrade took a drink of the tea. "Now, you don't bother your head about such inconsequentialities. If there was another bloke involved, he certainly made himself scarce this evening and so it would be nigh on impossible to pin anything on him. No, we are very happy to have caught two of the sharpest petermen in London, thanks to your help, Mr Holmes. From now on, however, it is a job for the professionals."

The young man gave a gracious nod of the head as though in some vague acquiescence to the wisdom of the Scotland Yarder. In reality he thought that, while Lestrade was not quite a fool, he was blinkered to the ramifications of the attempted robbery, and too easily pleased at landing a couple of medium-size fish in his net, while the really big catch swam free. Crime was never quite as cut and dried as Lestrade and his fellow professionals seemed to think. That was why this young man knew that he could never work within the constraints of the organised force as a detective. While at present he was reasonably content to be a help to the police, his ambitions lay elsewhere.

For his own part, Lestrade was unsure what to make of this lean youth with piercing grey eyes and gaunt, hawk-like features that revealed little of what he was thinking. There was something cold and impenetrable about his personality that made the inspector feel uncomfortable. In the last six months, Holmes had brought several cases to the attention of the Yard which he or his fellow officer, Inspector Gregson, had followed up, and a number of arrests had resulted. What Sherlock Holmes achieved from his activities, apart from the satisfaction every good citizen would feel at either preventing or solving a crime, Lestrade could not fathom. Holmes never spoke of personal matters, and the inspector was never tempted to ask.

At the same time as this conversation was taking place in Scotland Yard, in another part of the city the Professor was being informed of the failure of that night's operation at Meredith and Co. by his number two, Colonel Sebastian Moran.

The Professor rose from his chaise-longue, cast aside the mathematical tome he had been studying and walked to the window. Pulling back the curtains, he gazed out on the river below him, its murky surface reflecting the silver of the moon.

"In itself, the matter is of little consequence," he said, in a dark, even voice. "Merely a flea-bite on the body of our organisation. But there have been rather too many of these flea-bites of late. They are now beginning to irritate me." He turned sharply, his eyes flashing with anger. "Where lies the incompetence?"

Moran was initially taken aback by so sudden a change in the Professor's demeanour. "I am not entirely sure," he stuttered.

The Professor's cruelly handsome face darkened with rage. "Well, you should be, Moran. You should be sure. It is your job to know. That is what you are paid for."

"Well... it seems that someone is tipping the police off in advance."

The Professor gave a derisory laugh. "Brilliant deduction, Moran. Your public-school education has stood you in good stead. Unfortunately, it does not take a genius to arrive at that rather obvious conclusion. I had a visit from Scoular earlier this evening, thank goodness there is *one* smart man on whom I can rely."

At the mention of Scoular's name, Moran blanched. Scoular was cunning, very sharp and very ambitious. This upstart was gradually worming his way into the Professor's confidence, assuming the role of court favourite; consequently, Moran felt his own position in jeopardy. He knew there was no demotion in the organisation. If you lost favour, you lost your life also.

"What did he want?"

"He wanted nothing other than to give me information regarding our irritant flea. Apparently, he has been using the persona of Harry Jordan. He's been working out of some of the East End alehouses, The Black Swan in particular, where he latches on to our more gullible agents, like Johnson and Sims, and then narks to the police."

"What's his angle?"

Moriarty shrugged. "I don't know – or at least Scoular doesn't know. We need to find out, don't we? Put Hawkins on to the matter. He's a bright spark and will know what to do. Apprise him of the situation and see what he can come up with. I've no doubt Mr Jordan will return to his lucrative nest at The Black Swan within the next few days. I want information only. This Jordan character must not be harmed. I just want to know all about him before I take any action. Do you think you can organise that without any slip-ups?"

Moran clenched his fists with anger and frustration. He shouldn't be spoken to in such a manner – like an inefficient corporal with muddy boots. He would dearly have liked to wipe that sarcastic smirk off the Professor's face, but he knew that such a rash action would be the ultimate folly.

"I'll get on to it immediately," he said briskly, and left the room.

The Professor chuckled to himself and turned back to the window. His own reflection stared back at him from the night-darkened pane. He was a tall man, with luxuriant black hair and angular features that would have been very attractive were it not for the cruel mouth and the cold, merciless grey eyes.

"Mr Jordan," he said, softly addressing his own reflection, "I am very intrigued by you. I hope it will not be too long before I welcome you into my parlour."

Dawn was just breaking as Sherlock Holmes made his weary way past the British Museum and into Montague Street, where he lodged. He was no longer dressed in the cheap suit that he had used in his persona as Harry Jordan, but while his own clothes were less ostentatious, they were no less shabby. Helping the police as he did was certainly broadening his experience of detective work, but it did not put bread and cheese on the table or pay the rent on his two cramped rooms. He longed for his own private investigation – one of real quality. Since coming to London from university to make his way in the world as a consulting detective, he had managed to attract some clients, but they had been few and far between, and the nature of the cases – an absent husband, the theft of a brooch, a disputed will, and such like – had all been mundane. But, tired as he was, and somewhat dismayed at the short-sightedness of his professional colleagues at Scotland Yard, he did not waver in his belief that one day he would reach his goal and have a solvent and successful detective practice. And it needed to be happening soon. He could not keep borrowing money from his brother, Mycroft, in order to fund his activities.

He entered 14 Montague Street and made his way up the three flights of stairs to his humble quarters. Once inside, with some urgency he threw off his jacket and rolled up the sleeve of his shirt. Crossing to the mantelpiece, he retrieved a small bottle and a hypodermic syringe from a morocco leather case. Breathing heavily with anticipation, he adjusted the delicate needle before thrusting the sharp point home into his sinewy forearm, which was already dotted and scarred with innumerable puncture marks. His long, white, nervous fingers depressed the piston, and he gave a cry of ecstasy as he flopped down in a battered armchair, a broad, vacant smile lighting upon his tired features.